TRAVELLING ON LOVE IN A TIME OF UNCERTAINTY

TRAVELLING ON LOVE IN A TIME OF UNCERTAINTY

Contemporary Australian Gay Fiction

Editor

Gary Dunne

BlackWattle Press

Sydney Australia 1991

Some of the stories included here have appeared, in whole or in part, in *Campaign Australia, the Sydney Star Observer, OutRage,* or *Cargo.* BlackWattle Press would like to thank these publications, and their editors, for their support.

Published by BlackWattle Press
PO Box 4 Leichhardt NSW Australia 2040
September 1991

Printed by Southwood Press Marrickville NSW

Cover Art is a 1950's Pub painting, courtesy of the Trustees, Museum of Applied Arts and Sciences Sydney

ISBN 1.875243.06.2

Contents

Introduction

When I co-edited the anthology *Edge City on two different plans* back in 1983, I expected it to be the first of a new wave of Australian books from lesbian and gay perspectives. This country had both the writers and the readers, all that was missing was a publisher or two to fill the gap on the shelves.

A new wave did not, however, reach the beach until 1990. More gay and lesbian books were published in that one year than in the previous seven put together. 1991 looks like being even bigger. Most of these books are coming from smaller presses; such as *Designer Publications, BlackWattle Press* and *Hale and Iremonger.* Unlike overseas, our major publishers continue to be very wary of anything that isn't mainstream. Claire McNab's lesbian detective novels, pure Sydney North Shore, were hits in the US, then the UK, long before the Australian editions appeared. And it's not an isolated story. During the eighties, more of our gay and lesbian writers had their novels published overseas than in Australia.

Short story writers fared somewhat better during this period as both gay monthlies, *Campaign* and *OutRage*, have always published fiction. Under Dave Sargent's editorship in the late seventies, *Campaign* was the starting point for a number of literary careers. Sargent went on to play a central role in the development of a network of lesbian and gay writers and activists who edited and published a number of different journals and books in the early eighties.

Around that time in Melbourne, *OutRage* launched an annual short story competition which has since grown, both in terms of the number of entrants and the value of prizes offered. The Summer Literary Supplement issue in which the winners appear is consistently a best seller.

More recently, the *Star Observer,* Sydney's free gay newspaper, beefed up its summer issues with a selection of short stories, complementing their regular coverage of local books and writing.

Launched in 1988, *Cargo,* a non-commercial quarterly aimed at fostering poetry and prose from lesbian and gay perspectives, has expanded the overall amount of our work in print. Despite the notoriously short life spans of most small magazines, *Cargo* continues to grow in quality and circulation.

It's not surprising that this anthology is largely drawn from the best short stories that have appeared in each of these four publications over the past couple of years. Beyond our own press, gay stories continue to be very rare. Indeed, the situation hasn't changed much since the late seventies. While it's generally true that mainstream magazine editors don't discriminate against homosexual writers, it's also equally clear to those of us who are 'published occasionally' that they do discriminate against our submissions with overt gay content. Some gay (and, to a lesser extent, lesbian) writers lead double lives in print. Their gay identified stories appear in the gay press; their 'other' stories appear everywhere. From time to time a 'gay' story crosses over, but in general the usual venues for writers are closed if that writer chooses either to explore aspects of their sexuality or to deal with wider issues from a base that doesn't presuppose heterosexuality. It's a similar form of homophobia to that which pervades the local film and television industry. Debate about the validity of the label 'gay writing' obscures the issue of the ongoing invisibility of our writing in prevailing definitions of Australian literature.

The type of short story appearing in the gay press has changed since the early eighties. We've moved on from the monochrome coming out autobiographies concerned with the validation of sexual identity to a full spectrum of themes, literary styles and narrative sites. Contemporary gay fiction also reflects the profound influence, both personal and communal, of our years in the AIDS front-line. Having said that, it's tempting to go on and draw all kinds of conclusions based on the contents of this anthology, but a short story is not primarily a piece of sociology and these short stories quite eloquently speak for themselves. On the other hand, the choice of how and what to write can indicate much. Each story becomes a reference point on an overall map, a hearts and minds Australian gay guide.

As consumers of American and European gay fiction, we know a lot about where they live. We still see too little of our own territory and much of it remains as unknown to gay readers in the northern hemisphere as it is to too many Australian readers. This selection of stories, a view of where we live, is a small contribution to redressing those imbalances, both at home and away.

Gary Dunne
Editor

TONY AYRES

A Night Out with the Boys

It's Saturday night and I say to mum, "I'm going out with the boys."

She's in the kitchen, playing Mah Jong with the neighbours. She mumbles something disapproving in Chinese, but turns a lucky tile, and goes, "Ay yah!" The other ladies look at each other in disgust. Auntie Poong makes a nasty remark about the rips in my jeans, but I skip before someone tries to sew them up over the table like last time. Besides, my mum's on a winning streak, and Auntie Poong wants to bring her bad luck.

I meet Lewis after his shift at his dad's restaurant, and he smells like a stirfried chicken so I make him go home and shower before we hit the streets. Lewis and I are like chalk and cheese. I'm tall, gangly and skinny — Manchurian blood. I wear a leather jacket with metal badges pinned all over, crew cut and big boots. Lewis is a small, very pretty Chinese boy who dresses in tight jeans and braces.

I'm leaning against the walnut veneer, swigging his dad's Napoleon while he's blowdrying his hair and primping himself in the mirror. I tell him his perm makes him look like Lindy Chamberlain. He pokes his tongue out. The truth is Lewis and I only get on because we both love dancing and hate doing it alone.

We hit Patches, and it's the usual scene. Lewis knows all the Asian boys, and introduces me to Adrian, who is studying accounting at Sydney Uni. Adrian's dad runs a shoe factory in Kuala Lumpur, and he's telling me about the latest in Italian footwear while we watch the hunks cruise pass. Crepe soles bore me shitless so I make him buy me a beer, then grab Lewis and shimmy to the dance floor where Blackbox are playing *Ride on Time*. Lewis thinks he's Samantha Fox when he dances, all wobble and arse. Me, I'm more your Jerry Lewis type — spastic gyrations, and gratuitous bumping into things. But we have a lot of fun and work up a good sweat.

While we're recovering, a couple of middle aged rice queens come up to see how the paddy's growing. One's Phillip, who works in a PR company and loves Asian food. His friend Digby, is a librarian who wears Fletcher Jones. I get Digby, who remarks on how well I speak English. I say it's not too bad after 20 years of practice.

This Digby has been in the stacks too long. He rubs his knee against my thigh and tells me about his special Chinese friends. His Paco Raban is flooding my nostrils and I think I'm going to chuck, so I excuse myself, saying I need a piss. At the urinal, I think about all the other Digbys and our general incompatibility. Mostly they want to take me home and have me massage their feet, whereas I'd rather tie them up and fuck them with their mother's umbrella.

When I re-emerge Lewis, the cheap slut, is doing a sleazy Carmen number with Phillip, and Digby is discussing insteps and sole deodorisers with Adrian, so I decide it's time to fuck off.

I go to The Love Pump, this bookshop-cum-fuck-bar down the road. At the counter is a moustached throwback from Marlboro Country reading one of the Mills and Boon 'Doctor and Nurse' series. He gives me a dirty look when I ask to go into the backroom. I pay three bucks and fill out the 'membership' form, signing it 'Lee Kon You' — a little urological joke — then push the buzzer.

As I enter, everyone turns to check me out. I avert my gaze deferentially, like one of my fucking ancestors. I can't help it, it's in the blood.

The back part is divided into two rows of cubicles. The first begins just near the entrance; the second around the corner. They are connected by a circuitous corridor. Downstairs is another set of booths. I call that 'The Pits' because that's how you feel if you end up there. This place used to be pastel blue like some fru-fru apartment at Darling Point, but years of body fluids and cockroach shit have turned it into faggot purgatory.

I first came here with Robert two years ago. There were porno videos in the cubicles then, and locks on all the booths. Ah, the salad days! Like Robert, the place has gone to the grave. The doors in the second row are kicked in. Bits of rubble everywhere. It's a disgrace.

I skulk along the corridor through the dim blue light, pretending I'm looking for my kid brother or something and humming 'Hooray for Hollywood'. I don't know why I act this way. It's not conducive to getting your end in. Meanwhile I check out the talent. Most of the action is around the first row of cubicles near the entrance.

Waiting outside one of the booths is a dimpled, pug-nosed blonde, my age. He's tapping his Reeboks in time to the disco blaring over our heads, one hand slung over the crotch of his stonewash jeans. I bet he's called Brad. A body-width away, trying to cop a feel, is a chunky little guy who must work out a lot, but only comes up to Brad's armpit. Brad flinches and bumps his head against the wall. With a snort, he leaves this booth area and does a circuit around the corridor. Mighty Mouse follows him.

A weedy Spanish guy about fifty tries to feel my bum, but I'm interested in the one with the moustache next to him. He's thirtyish, got a bowl haircut, thick blonde fuzz over his lip and is wearing a t-shirt his mum picked up from K-Mart. But his jeans are 501's, so maybe there's hope. Besides, there's an expression of utter terror in his eyes which turns me on no end. He's looking my way. I look back.

A porno-star, hunky-chunky, brunette boy slides out of the booth Brad was waiting on. His white t-shirt is hanging out the back pocket of skintight, savagely ripped 501's. This guy is Butch with a capital 'B'. With a lazy flick, he sweeps the sweat off his torso, fondling his nipple on the way. The booths on either side of him empty out. From the left, an exhausted young sailor staggers out the exit, gripping his buttocks. On the right, two mauve-coloured men with blow-waves clutch each other and roll their eyeballs. Sexy looks at them like they are some lower form of life.

"Enjoy the show, girls?"

They giggle and titter like chooks around the cock.

Sexy checks who else he wants. There's me, my friend with the moustache and sleazy old Pablo Picasso, slouched against the wall with a fag hanging out his bottom lip. Sexy decides to try around the corridor.

Just as he turns out of sight, Brad comes the other way, hotly pursued by Mighty Mouse. He sees the open door of Sexy's cubicle, and his face drops with disappointment. Who'd blame him? He follows around the corridor. So does Mighty Mouse.

Meanwhile, I'm casting intermittent glances of intense lust towards the Moustache. I decide this is enough foreplay, and make a beeline for him, putting my hand somewhere obvious, like his dick. To my chagrin, he pushes it away. Feeling stung, I go around the corridor.

Back there, a pile of other blokes are hanging about like

scarecrows in the dark. Leaning against walls and corners, gliding past each other in slow motion, as if they were moving through water. It's indigo blue and whispery, and suddenly I'm wondering what life must be like at the bottom of the ocean. Nevertheless, I'm keeping my feelers peeled for someone half-decent who is willing to be seduced by my slant-eyed charms. Some nights are OK. Others you feel like the leper at the charity ball. Tonight's one of them. This 'jogger' (ha ha) looks at me like I should get back on the boat. I would have kicked him up the butt-plug except I notice, cruising in like a U-boat, the venerable Moustache. He stops at a respectable distance and looks my way.

I maintain my dignity this time and lean against the wall with my legs spread. It's up to him to make the move. Old Romeo, though, just leans back himself and picks at something encrusted on his left nostril. This could be a long night.

I make a move to depart. My leisure time is more valuable than this. Besides, there's a sudden drift back to the first cubicles which can only mean one thing. Sexy and Brad are getting it on.

When I get there, they are lolling their tongues around each other's earholes. Sexy rips Brad's shirt open, which causes the fifteen men crammed around them to simultaneously tremble at the knee. I wouldn't mind a peak at this blue-blood myself, but can only see black curls and blonde flat top between the wedge of other bodies. I'd be better off watching bloody Charles and Di on telly. Anyway, Sexy and Brad get sick of these less-than-perfect hands tainting their more-than-perfect bods, so they duck into the far cubicle. There's a rush for next door. Mighty Mouse bullies his way through, God bless him. The crowd disperses. Loud groaning sounds rumble off the walls and echo like pornography through the thin blue air. In time to the music, too. Fucking show-offs!

At the other end, observing these shenanigans, is the Moustache, wearing a smile which you could only describe as wry.

I think, "Just my luck, he's a fucking intellectual."

He stares remorselessly into my pinched brown eyes with those wide baby blues, and it occurs to me that I'm in love. There's nothing I wouldn't do for this specimen. Sometimes it just happens like that.

Pablo is still in his corner, huffing and puffing in time to the Pet Shop Boys. It's not a flattering sight. I slide into the booth directly in front of my man, leaving the door tantalisingly ajar.

It's small in there. With two it's like bonking in a toothpaste tube, but I'm young and supple and good at making the most out of tight spaces. But Moustache doesn't accept the direct invitation. Instead someone enters the booth to my right. I kneel and peer through the hole the size of a large jam jar, situated ever so conveniently at groin height. To my great disappointment, I do not find a thirty year old Moustache awaiting me through the porthole of love. I find a fifty year old, greasy Pablo Picasso blowing smoke mere centimetres from me. I grab my jacket and abandon ship.

Outside, the Moustache is engrossed with proceedings at the other end. Brad and Sexy's booth is rocking violently, which sends a shiver through the entire block. There's an unrestrained howl of abandon, and a constant thump, thump, thump, like a heartbeat on its way to a massive coronary. A number of guys are loitering nearby, desperate for a whiff when the lovebirds blow. I think this is shameless.

The Moustache shrugs his shoulders and smiles enigmatically. By now, I am convinced he is a genius. He heads down the stairs to the Pits, and without missing a beat, I follow.

It is a regular coalmine down there except for the pale moon through the barred windows and the occasional orange glow of a cigarette tip. Pablo has followed us and makes an unsolicited bid for my bum. I get this unexpected, fierce urge to whack him, but manage to restrain myself. Instead, I suggest that he might like to go stuff an enchilada or words to that effect.

Against a back wall I make out the Moustache's outline. Fortunately, he has severely slumped shoulders so you can't miss him. As I head towards his shadow, he pops into a booth and locks the door; prickteasing motherfucker. But what can you do when Cupid plays on your heart strings? I go into the cubicle next to his.

I'm kneeling and he's kneeling and there's a thin masonite partition between us. All that permits our love is this little window. It's thrillingly romantic.

"Hi, I'm Geoffrey," he whispers.

"Simon."

"Simon, that's an unusual name."

"What did you expect . . . Charlie Chan?"

He laughs, then coughs in a dry fit.

OK, he's no Einstein. That's not so bad. I am also heavily turned on by low levels of intelligence.

"You have a most unusual sense of dress, Simon. It looks good."

I might be in love, but I haven't got all night. I decide to go to the heart of the matter.

"You are a really attractive man, Simon," he babbles.

"That's very nice mate, but do you want to suck my cock or what?"

Geoffrey lights a cigarette, and through the flicker of his Bic lighter, I see how shagged out he looks — the pock marks on his cheeks, the black rings under his eyes, the scabby blotches around his neck.

"You don't know how much I'd love to, Simon, but I have to be honest. I came here tonight because I was desperate to talk to someone. You probably think that's silly."

I'm thinking it is fucking criminal as well as indescribably stupid. Where does he think he is, the Salvation Army? Then he starts hacking again for a longer time. I remember where I've seen those blotches before. Jesus fuck, why do I get all the luck?

"Sorry . . . " he says, weakly, " . . . sorry. You probably want to go back."

"No," I say, lying through my teeth, "Actually, it's cute meeting someone who doesn't kiss on the first date. I've always been an easy lay myself . . . "

Geoffrey chuckles. My face is close enough to the wall to feel his bony fingers. My impulse is to run like hell but for some reason I grab his hand. He tells me about what it's like in the Department of Waterworks. Growing up in Coffs Harbour. Bird watching in the Blue Mountains. Solitude in a small flat in Epping. I'm thinking all this time, "What am I doing here?" but my hand's glued to his like A and B Araldite. I hear about Sonya, the daughter. Nine years old, going to be a real stunner.

I've held a skinny hand like that before, you know. My first boy. His name was Robert. He loved rap-music. It's amazing, but I bet you never knew that you can feel a heartbeat through a thumb. Or that you can sense the race of blood along the arteries through someone's palm. You can feel the liver, the intestines, the lungs. You just have to be a little sensitive to it. I touch them all in this Geoffrey's lonely grasp. All that blood and shit whirling around out of control. Wild blood. Out of control.

When I get back home I find that my reckless mum has just about gambled away my inheritance. She's in a black mood. Auntie Poong is tucking into some candied chicken's feet, grinning like a lizard at noon. Mum starts abusing me in Chinese for coming home so late. She says I've caused her all this bad luck, that I've made her hair go grey. She even waves her false teeth in my direction as if they were my fault too. Mrs Kim is telling her to get on with the game.

I wait till she pops her gams back in, and kiss her on the cheek goodnight. Then I go to my room, light a stick of incense and pray that the Dead are at peace. I'm not even sure if this is a proper religion, but it's what my mum taught me.

I remember Geoffrey's phone number and pull it out of my back pocket. 357 something. I chuck it in the bin.

In bed, I stare at the ceiling, feeling agitated and angry about something. I wonder if, maybe, I should have punched that Spanish guy? A good smack to the chops. Whack! I drift into sleep, thinking about what would have happened if I had. The commotion. The blood. The sound of bone on flesh. Bone. Flesh. Whack!

KERRY BASHFORD

The Suicide Scrapbook

The story I am about to tell you is one you may have already heard. It involves a man who was so disenchanted with the little life had to offer that he decided to offer up his own life. He tied a noose to a tree bough at the edge of a cliff. He swallowed poison and held a revolver to his temple. The gun misfired, severing the rope around his neck. Drowning and gasping in the sea below, he threw up the lethal dose. An officious lifeguard nearby delivered the man to the relative safety of the beach. It is not known whether he repeated the attempt.

I have, for some time now, kept a scrapbook of newspaper reports of suicide. I'm not entirely sure why I've done this. I guess it's natural for someone in my position to have an interest in matters of mortality. I'm simply intrigued by the lengths to which some people go to make their next breath their last.

I've been spared the responsibility of plotting my own destruction. This I've left in the hands of a modern microorganism. It's true, I once had a romantic notion of dying by my own hands. But in the end, it wasn't tenacity or an indestructible life force that kept the boy breathing. Instead, it was simple curiosity. How much, I wondered, could one body endure before succumbing to the inevitable?

It's a fascination my doctor shares. My medical history is at the point of becoming serialised. I'm pleased that I can be such a diversion for him. It seems after all these years, I've finally found a man who truly appreciates my body.

It's Tuesday. At least, I think it is. Simon is wandering around my flat, preparing lunch, propping up pillows, emptying ashtrays. He's been visiting me regularly since my last visit to the hospital. I've been thinking of asking for a replacement. Someone who's a little less efficient and a little more entertaining.

Today, he seems more preoccupied than usual. I ask

him, what's wrong? He says, nothing. I say, it's rude to lie to a dying man, so tell me, you little fuck. He says, I'm having problems with my boyfriend . . . it's nothing, really . . . it's really very trivial.

What he means is that it must seem trivial compared to my plight. What he doesn't realise is that I crave the trivial, the unimportant. Just once I'd like a conversation that isn't prefaced by the question . . . and how are you today? Just once I'd like a conversation of absolutely no consequence.

Fuck it, what I want is a good gossip, okay.

It's still Tuesday. Alex pays me a visit. I don't know why Alex pays me a visit. He certainly never did when I was able bodied. He's sitting at the edge of my bed watching me, studying me.

He says, I have read that there is a tendency in those with terminal illnesses to eroticise their disease, do you think this is true? I say, I don't know. He says, well, think about it. I say, I will.

And I do. All afternoon. I imagine that my immune system is playing host to a cannibalistic horde who, at the point of climax, devour each other like praying mantises.

I'm not sure this is what he meant.

Alex has left me a magazine that carries a report of a New York performance artist who apparently filmed himself dismembering his erect penis with an axe.

God, what people will do to get into pictures. Coming soon to a theatre near you.

It's Wednesday morning 2.30am. I've just watched the late movie with Joan Crawford in which she loses her husband to the war, only to find that he has left behind a string of lovers and a mountain of debts. To make matters worse, her daughter, her only child, is dying of an incurable disease. It was a rare tropical one, I think. At the time, I thought this was rather odd seeing as they lived in Connecticut.

So there she was faced with the loss of her family and her fortune. Did she give in? Did she reach for the razor blade? No, not Joan. God, the bitch was so brave. Barely even a quiver from those monumental eyebrows.

Wednesday afternoon. There is a knock at the door. From the next room, I can hear Paul's voice. I try to conceal my excitement as he ushers Simon out of the house. He then creeps to my bedside and conjures from his satchel, a bottle of OP rum.

Over the following hours, we cuddle in front of the heater. At least, Paul still thinks I'm good for a cuddle. We once tried to be lovers but neither of us could stop laughing.

It's a wonderful afternoon. Paul tells me all the sordid tales from the outside world. I have not felt such an exquisite wickedness since I smoked cigarettes in the school toilets and played with my classmates' willies in the same venue. It's worth it, the next day, when Simon nurses me through the most horrific hangover I have ever endured. It's even worth his lectures on temperance when he discovers the empty bottle beside my bed.

Honestly, a man in your condition.

It's Thursday. I'm alone. And the television is conspiring against me.

Thus begins my manifesto.

Death to all soap opera stars and all other specimens of American dentistry.

Death to all used car salesmen and all those promoted to quiz show hosts.

Death to all those who populate children's shows, who smile and cajole and never let the little fuckers know what they're in for.

Most of all, death to Mrs Marsh.

A pox on you all. My pox on you all.

And when some clumsy cleaner polishes the wrong button and hurtles our species into oblivion, it will not be a moment too soon.

It has not been a good day.

There was one bright moment however. In today's paper, I found an article about a man who wrapped himself in a wet electric blanket and threw on the switch. I was tremendously impressed by this. I think it shows such an innovative approach to death. Not to mention domestic appliances.

Alex sits at the edge of my bed. He says, isn't the phallus an extraordinary thing, it has the power to attract and command, it has been the cause of many wars and will be the cause of many more.

I say, exactly how long have you held your cock in such high regard?

He says, dying seems to suit your temperament well, do you think this is true? I say, I don't know. He says, well think about it. I say, I will.

And I do. And perhaps he's right. Maybe I should use the little time I have left to become a nice person.

Meanwhile, hell freezes over, pigs fly and I live to a ripe old age.

My reign of terror commences on Friday morning at approximately 11 o'clock. Before Simon can even set foot in the bedroom, I launch into a rage that alarms even myself. Simon places a meal on my lap and sneaks out of the door while I'm in mid sentence.

I go through my address book and accost my friends and acquaintances. Two hours later, there is a knock at the door. It's Paul. He slaps me across the face.

With this one blow, Paul has given me back one thing that I have lost during my period of illness. He has returned to me the right that we all share — to be beaten severely around the face and neck. I have at last been given permission to be punished.

It's the following week and Simon refuses to look me in the eye. I'm not surprised after my performance on Friday.

He walks away from me, his hand cupped to his face. I call him back and pat the bed beside me. I gently hold his face against my chest.

I say, I'm sorry, I really didn't mean those things I said. He says, I know, you see, Robert's left me and I don't know what to do.

I'm not really sure myself. I've never been very good at marriage counselling. So I simply rock him back and forth, back and forth, for a few minutes.

And I tell him about last night. You see, last night, it almost happened. Last night, I almost bit the big one. As I lay in my bed, I didn't think of impending death. I didn't think of all the family and friends I would leave behind. All I could think about was that the next day, my corpse was going to be found in an untidy room. I got out of my death bed and struggled and swayed for a few minutes, trying to reorganise the mess. Finally, I collapsed at the foot of my bed.

I was relieved to wake up this morning. At least, I saved the coroner the difficulty in explaining exactly why the body was found lying naked, face down on the floor, with a feather duster in his hand.

It has now been two weeks since I last defied death. There have been no new entries into my scrapbook. This is not through lack of interest or material, but because Simon has found it and it has been duly confiscated. What Simon doesn't realise is that I'm preparing a new volume that I will compile as soon as I can convince Paul to buy me some paste. If not, I'll be reduced to flour and water. Simon says that if I don't behave myself, I'll be reduced to bread and water.

Simon maintains that I shouldn't have such a morbid preoccupation. But I can't help it. I feel such an affinity with these people, such an admiration for them. I have more than a cursory knowledge of the process of dying and I know that it is, like life, no place for sissies.

But maybe I should find another hobby. I could content myself with collecting opportunistic illnesses. I seem to have a flair for this. Or perhaps I could collect stamps.

Nah.

BENEDICT CIANTAR

Whorin' at the Horden

I'm sitting by myself in the corner of the room. There are thousands of people everywhere and I've had an ecy so I'm really out of it. I'm just sitting there, watching and observing everybody. My body is buzzing. I feel as though I am the most gorgeous man in the room. People strut by with similar notions. There is a boy in front of me wearing thin black footy shorts and no underpants, black boots. His crotch is huge and as he dances it flops from side to side. He knows I am watching. The show is for me. A friend of a friend dances by, arms around his flatmate, a wink, I almost see light reflect from his teeth. The boy in front seems to be getting an erection. I move my chair, adjust position as if uncomfortable, spreading my legs. He is directly in front now. Beneath the constant thud I hear a familiar baseline. Adeva's *Respect?* No . . . Over my friend's shoulder I notice two men I am obsessed with. Both are in their early thirties. They are Sydney's Tom of Finland. The shortest one is cutest. He is wearing his usual attire; running shoes, footy shorts, old sweaty t-shirt. His boyfriend in blue jeans, shirtless. I fantasize of living with them in their apartment, the three of us happy . . . I glare at them hoping they will notice me. Nothing. My friend with the erection seems to have found someone else to play with. That baseline again. I rush down onto the dance floor. My pelvis is loose, it swings and thrusts with ease. My little friend appears from nowhere. Don't be too obvious. I turn my back on him and casually move closer. I can almost feel his crotch against my arse. I am horny as hell. I pull out my bottle and take a huge sniff through each nostril. A tap on the shoulder. It is amazing how many friends you discover when in possession of a bottle of amyl. Both of us are spinning. We dance hard and long, crotches rubbing to the music. I am so horny that I could almost take him on the dance floor this very second. Slowly I become aware of the surroundings. Not wanting to be too tacky I move slightly away.

Arms around my waist, "We've been lookin' for you

everywhere!" My flatmate and friends. "Wanna go outside for a while?"

Now!?

I contemplate the thought for a second as if unsure. I also notice that my friend in the black shorts has found someone else.

"Yeah. Why not."

We weave our way through the crowd, hand in hand, to the edge of the dance floor. There are lots of people standing around. There is a man sitting over against the wall by himself. Boots and blue jeans, bare chest, huge and hairless. He is beautiful. My stomach churns. I cannot feel my feet. My legs are numb. I am floating.

It is a hot night. I look for a patch of grass to sit on. There are lots of people everywhere. Lots of semi-naked bodies, bulging crotches, bare shaven chests . . . I tell Emma about the guy in the shorts.

"Do you want to go back in hon?"

"No, no. Didn't like that song much anyway."

My feelings have changed. No longer am I sexy. There is too much competition. No longer do I love everyone. There is too much pretentiousness. I start to feel contemplative. The two Tom of Finland clones are over by the bar. I watch them for a while. Who are they? What are they doing? But it is still early and I cannot afford to get depressed.

"I need to move."

"Oh . . . " She does not want to.

Regardless, we return inside, back to the crowds and the sweaty bodies. Back to distraction.

It is dawn. My body refuses to give in. I have been dancing for a good eight hours. Endlessly moving and thrashing about. Constantly perving and searching. There are still at least three thousand people here. What on earth is everybody doing? While the rest of the world sleeps these few thousand people insist on defying all sense of logic, all sensibility. Most of my friends have gone home but I cannot commit myself to leave, I may miss something. The music has slowed to a funky seventies beat. Only the hard core party animals remain. (Me?) We scream and hoot for another hour or so.

Slowly I find boredom. Slowly I discover reality.

It is a strange thing strolling home at eight in the morning. The air is misty and fresh, grass wet and green. Signs of life become apparent. Newspapers strewn across sparkling lawns, a lone jogger blindly obsessed, the occasional push-bike rider glides silently down the street, the distant growl of a garbage truck collecting its last load. It is an effort to walk, a struggle to move. Emma and I discuss highlights. Like the couple we saw fucking high up in the stands, and the man I danced with clad in only his y-front jockeys, of snorting amyl and spinning out in a haze of smoke . . . 'Wasn't it great the way they mixed Adeva's *Respect* with Aretha Franklin's?' 'Yeah, I just went wild.'

We arrive back at the house. Our flatmates are all in bed but the kitchen is full with people. A friend and a friend and their friends . . . We drink coffee and smoke cigarettes for hours. Story after story of the night and what it held. The music, the lights, the decorations, the stupid drag shows . . . By midday I feel myself tiring. I wish these people would leave, I need to sleep. The party is over. Go home! Nobody seems to be aware, or even care that they are in somebody else's home. Hints are dropped. As the hours drag I become less subtle. The chatter continues. Eventually I go to bed leaving Emma to cope with it all.

It is almost 1.30pm and the sun attacks my bed with viciousness and contempt. I pull the blinds, strip and crawl under the sheet. No music today. Silence is bliss.

As I wake I am confronted with a confusing image. Complete darkness. I look to my clock for clarity, 6.25pm. Then I remember . . . There is a faint but constant thud rising from below. My bedroom bounces and shakes. Surely they are not playing dance music! I become increasingly confused and immediately angered. The lounge room contains at least ten people. I enter, turn and leave, their laughter echoing in my head. The kitchen, as usual is a complete mess. I try to ignore the overflowing ashtrays and garbage bins. I cannot bring myself to return to the lounge room. Do they not have a home to go to? Have they not slept? I am boiling the kettle as Emma finds her way into the kitchen.

In disbelief, "I came downstairs and they were all just sitting there."

"Haven't they been home yet?" I ask, realizing it's the same crowd I left here five and a half hours prior.

"No. They've just been sitting in our lounge room all day."

"Fucking hell!" I am ropable. "These people amaze me."

But don't be angry, I tell myself. This is Darlinghurst after all.

KOSTA MATSOUKAS

Trick or Treat

He had described the desired body over the phone. Young, but not puppyish, firm but not rock-hard; full lips important.

The attitude, very important. Responsive to subtle direction rather than docile. No costume, no toys. Safe, goes without saying.

He sat back lighting a cigarette way ahead of the time at which one was due, (one hourly intervals which he mostly kept to . . . mostly).

How could the guy, how could anyone have sex for money?

What do you do if you can't find anything about the client that turns you on? What if there wasn't anything about himself . . . ? Not that he's bad-looking, he's just not spectacular, that's all. He is surprised by how important it is that the boy likes him.

He doesn't really give a damn; if the boy doesn't like him he'll just have to pretend. That's his job aint it? *He* has to sell himself at the office every day, hasn't he? He gets his scrotum stretched regularly by that insufferable General Manager don't he? We all have to suffer and to make suffer, it can't be avoided.

But suffering isn't the point. Is he feeling vindictive? The point is to have a great fuck like the one before. Sure, a little suffering has helped in the past. It did with the blonde. He wants this to be as good as the one with the blonde. Better! One perfect hour. He needs a drink to make himself ready. He pours a drink.

Bullshit! He doesn't need a drink. He should have had a bath. He'll wait so they can have a drink together, break the ice. Will the boy be nervous? He should have stocked up the bar. It'll be fine.

The doorbell! He can see his outline through the glass door. He's taller than he wanted! Didn't he mention size? Opens

the door all ready to piss him off. Mmm . . . Think again. He's
got the lips alright. It'll be a great pity if he doesn't kiss. Nice
eyes, too. Will he keep them closed? He hopes he won't. Hopes
he'll be looking him straight in the eye, especially when he
mounts. But you can't ask for that. You can't say 'Don't turn
your goddamn face away as if I was ridiculous.' Please look at
me. Please don't look at me. It doesn't really make a differ-
ence.

The young man says 'Hello there,' steps inside, waits to
be told to sit down. Maybe he doesn't mind being kissed now?

He walks in, strides over to the sofa and sits on the arm,
lights a cigarette.

'Nice pad you got here mister. Nice packet too. You
wanna check mine out?'

Ooops, no, that's too fast. Business first, pleasure after.
How much, how long, how good? It's all relative of course. No
it's not. 'Would you like a drink?' No.

-Wanna drink?

-Yes, thanks.

The young guy takes off his jacket. Then his boots.
That'll do for now. He is just sitting, looking alert and inviting,
waiting. Are you anxious, nervous? I should tell him now. 'Look
I think you are very good-looking, it's just that you are bigger
than I expected.' Get real! Just tell him you like it slow. He
hands the young man a drink.

-Here, that'll relax you.

-Cheers.

He sips. He gulps.

-So, what have you got to show me?

-Come here pal.

God, the boy's an idiot; or else, he's certainly inexper-
ienced!

-No, just show me.

He takes off his t-shirt, still sitting, slides it off with both
hands, nicely executed, brilliant androgynous tits, round and
firm with upright, well-trained nipples.

I take all in while at the same time watching his young
obliging face. He's confident, good, there shouldn't be any
problems.

He is scanning my face for signs of approval.

Exhibitionist slut! Lovely.

He sees I am pleased; he isn't waiting any more, he walks
over slowly. Stands close but doesn't touch. Undoes his belt
and holds it with a kind of tender threat before he lets it slide
on the floor. He knows what he is doing. Maybe he knows the

blonde.

He undoes his fly and bends down to take his trousers to his ankles. Is he bowing? He is not too close. For the brief moment when I cannot monitor his expression I take in his shapely back, the smooth nape of the neck. He is waiting again. I will him to touch me. He raises his arm, puts his hand at the back of my neck and gently gets hold of a tuft of hair. He does nothing, he is just standing there. He says:

-Do you want to do it here?

I take him by the hand and lead him to the bedroom. 'What do you like? . . . Have you been doing this long? . . . ' We say nothing.

There is a mirror on the side of the bed. This should be interesting. Nice. A good session. Lovely.

But the john is slightly nervous.

-Another drink?

-Maybe later.

-Let's get a bit comfortable. Here, let me slip this off.

Nice. Don't do anything. There.

Lie next to him with just a little body-pressure equally distributed. Kiss him on the sternum. The nipple. A small suck. Put each hand on his waist. He likes *this*. Knead a bit, massage his abdomen. Yes, that's good, let yourself go. No worries.

Undo the belt, get on with it, I want to get under those covers pretty soon, I'm getting chilly. Slide his trousers off. Good timing, he's getting hard. Brush him there. A bit more. Now move away, fine. Now lips, no tongue yet. More nipples. *Now* tongue. OK he's hard. He's not hard enough yet. He's ready. Make him show he wants it. They always let you know when they want it.

It's fast. He lays me out and slides into me strong and hard, hungrily; a good thing I made myself ready, he liked watching that too. So did I; that mirror is perfectly placed.

It's slow. He wants me on top and is waiting for me to guide him. There you go, gently does it, is it hot and tight enough for you? I don't mind it a bit myself, just no wild thrusting just yet, give me half a minute. Goood.

-I can tell you've got a sense of rhythm.

Sometimes you have to plaster yourself to the bastards to stop them from ripping you in two. I don't mind being ridden as long as they realize I don't need breaking in as well.

It's a great fit! You can tell he likes it by the way he lifts himself and then slides back down on it. He likes me to watch.

-Bend over and kiss me. Stick your tongue down my

throat. Now lean back and pinch your tits.

Perfect!

-Do you like what I'm doing to you? What are you sitting on? You get off on getting cock up your ass, don't you? You know you like it. Tell me what you like.

God the man's a talker!

It wasn't like that. They never even made it to the bedroom. They did it on the living room floor, quickly and efficiently. A few thrusts and a muffled grunt. Once he was inside he couldn't stop himself from coming. They had another drink and then the young guy left.

It wasn't like that either. They fucked on the living room floor as well as in the bedroom, staring into each other's eyes most of the time. They took turns in mounting and mouthing one another on impulse with several breaks in between for drinks and cigarettes. Condoms strewn where they had rolled. They came together to their surprise, and stayed cradling for a long time afterwards.

They didn't come but neither cared. They fell asleep with happy expectations of more sex when they woke up, before going out to look for a place together.

It wasn't like that at all. They only set eyes on each other once in a crowded train. A month later neither of them would know it if they tripped over each other.

Sailor Cray

It's D-Day on the strand before Vaucluse House. Three able-bodied seamen pile out of a water taxi, bottles of Moet under all available arms. Sailor Cray leads them on, looking like a lubber as he swings me a drunken grin.

I'm sitting next to Josef on a picnic rug. Today's birthday boy has big tears reflecting sunlight just like the harbour. Josef's boyfriend hasn't showed or even sent a card. Gone to Lord Howe Island with another man, whisper the queens in aspic.

There's 30 of us — an assortment of genders, winging our way on cold turkey and gossip late in the afternoon. I suggest someone change the tape, put on something more cheery than Patsy Cline as Josef is very depressed.

"Let's have champagne," roars Sailor Cray, who rubs the curly top of Josef's head with a free hand and then performs the same on me. "Hello," he says and staggers to his knees. He then turns and kisses each and every girl on the rug. A straight man on land.

Things are different in the submarine. The boys hug close down there and the submariner is the true democrat. Officers are on the level and if gay slurs wash their way from Salerno to Frisco, undersea buddies will always stand by their poofter mate. Sailor Cray told me such stories from the very beginning. Then other things surfaced too, and behind the flash of vanity from his blue-fish eyes, I gleaned a run of hearts in every port. Guess my dock had come around now.

I met him through Julia, the mad hipoid with the astral gaze. She drafted up my chart in the beer garden of the Lord Nelson.

"Oh, you've got everything," she declared. "A Gemini with bits of fire and water. And then there's Jupiter in the midheaven. Such a beautiful balance."

Julia had brought her cousin from California along, a part Cherokee Indian with perfect teeth, and brain drain.

"Matt is so gorgeous. Don't you like Matt my beautiful man?" "Beautiful," was always the word on Julia's lips and she felt psychic about the two of us, suggesting that a romantic horoscope was quite in order. My eyes meantime were hunting a certain bar stool. The tawny sailor gathered me in through the base of his schooner glass.

They called him Cray because of his tight body and spidery arms. "Crayfish" enjoyed a tight squeeze. Just like a lobster in a tank he would haul himself up, high over the heads and shoulders of his mates feeling out for stray wires or loose connections in the crannies of the sub.

He almost crawled off the bar stool to come over, offering a crusty palm and dropping a pair of hundred dollar bills in the gesture. Julia picked them up, muttered that he couldn't be an earth sign being so careless with money. Cray just pulled out another bill and bought cocktails for everyone. Then he complained about star signs being the curse of Sydney life:

"They're an instant character assassination, you know."

"Bad karma to mock the stars," said Julia

"Bad taste too," said Julia's cousin, shrugging a tic of malice onto Cray's soiled overalls.

Bad taste has bolder designs I figured, especially after Cray jettisoned me off to his apartment at Darling Point. But the sticky gum tree oils and clamouring urchins, the framed photograph of Cray dressed Dutch at an Edam cheese factory were tossed over. Just a trivial drift of ocean next to Cray, the coral cay of a lovemaker.

Hard to fathom how ten years inside the cold, steel tube of a sub had not dampened Cray's hot-blooded gift of sex. Then again, perhaps the navy was what had spawned it, where raw dreams of passion found their carnal truth on land.

Neither of us was concerned with peak performance, though we hit the Blue Mountains on the same afternoon. Cray wanted to get right away from the sea. Ten years in the service and his wallet busting out with super, he dictated our kip and Balmoral House with its twin-set of giant canopied beds, filigree lace curtains and Victorian lamps in ruby glass gave us all the preliminaries for a night of high style fucking.

Cray possessed a holy sadhu's view about orgasm, so he worked his way up, splaying our bodies at wild angles, thrusting and taking us of in a spirited caress.

"Climax takes something from your soul you know."

'Divine semen,' I wondered, though I wasn't prepared to argue. Nor was I prepared for the alarm bells at eight o'clock.

An ambulance or a car alarm maybe, but Cray gave up the sensual touch in an instant, pushed me off and looked almost ready to weep.

"What the hell's the matter."

A iron hard torso knocked the post and sent the canopy at sea. Cray rolled off into the bathroom. A flush of tears without words.

I suppose I didn't care enough back then. Regarded Cray as just another neurotic carrying the fleshy pink cross of sexual guilt. Being boy wonder in the cot was a contradiction. I knew well that the real gay persona never revealed itself until sex was over.

I ate dinner alone, feeling almost cocooned in the silk and gossamer decor. The bill would still be on Cray so I doubled up on entrees for novices. After the medallions of venison, came smoked eel, but the aroma linked up with Cray's own unusual body smell. I opted for the smoking room instead where the glow of open logs sizzled my short term memory for crimson passion. Meanwhile, Cray's ice-blue sub kept drifting in and fanning out the flames.

"Sorry. I'm very sorry. There's been a death in the family."

Cray had showered and changed, as the wide and endearing grin had come back with a sparkling vengeance.

"My father died last year," I muttered ineffectually, as Cray walked off again.

He returned with a carafe of port and a pair of brandy balloons. A production line of deep and relentless guzzling was rearing.

Cray had been in the dining room, inviting each guest to come and share log and conversation space. The suggestion was jovial and civilised, and almost 20 people trained their way along, caught under the influence of those sailor blue eyes.

He rolled off the introductions with gusto, inscribed each name and took centre posse on the settee. Cray loved to dictate everything though now and then some words would sweep beyond him.

"Where are your girls tonight?" The skinny husband was asking.

"Girls mean trouble," said Cray, shuffling his big feet and shaking off the lobster hue. "Ten years in the navy taught me that."

The skinny husband looked relieved. "Maybe later," he said.

But his wife pulled us back to the straight and now.

"Mountain girls have fine complexions."

"Forget it," I said, playing brash and risky, "Cray's in love with a mermaid."

At least the skinny husband gave a laugh. Cray ignored my prod and drafted conversation back to the undersea:

"I'm just happy to breath the air up here. Ten years in a sub and you forget what the world really smells like."

"It must smell awful," added someone, "being cooped up with all those sweaty men."

Cray anchored the memory. "Unwashed bodies is what you get used to. It's the way civilians smell which is a bother. So clean, scrubbed and clinical. When you first come back up on land it unnerves you. Something like bodies in a morgue."

"Ooh," said a solo voice.

The rest of the audience were silent and expectant for Cray's ramble had opened hatches. The impervious naval ego buckling under the pressure. None of us could read the dials of course so Cray took the leeway, threw up his glass to me and beckoned uncomfortably for more.

After skolling the entire balloon of port Cray began to stagger.

"The lads are dead," he cried out.

They all looked at Cray as if this was a metaphor for his missing the navy.

"Why not go back to it Cray," came a reassuring voice.

"I think we'd better get him to bed," I said, for Cray had crashed out on the settee.

When morning came, Cray was right back to normal. Even rolled back the sheets on the opposite twin in order to fool the maid. Another gay cover I wondered or just something perverse about Cray. Ocean boys have everyone fishing for secrets.

We snuck along the corridor, our bellies glued over with semen. Cray jostled for space under the shower, though like everything else, I knew he was desperate to share. Bodies and booze had become mutual life-supports.

In the Paragon Cafe we drank chocolate while Cray conversed with more strangers. Cray gleaned surfaces as I scaled hard for souls, especially that strategic rock of his own.

"A death in the family," was what Cray had said. My first mode of attack had Cray looking disturbed:

"I didn't mean my real family," he said.

An intrusion on the Paragon's perfunctory mood.

"So who died then?"

"Let's call it a nightmare at sea," said Cray, reaching for an innocent tone.

He was always speaking in symbols or riddles and it puzzled how those earthy lads had ever dealt with such an enigma.

A nightmare. My mind scanned every possibility. Giant squids to Moby Dick and there was always the now common-place — dolphins in driftnets, poison algae suffocating the waterways. But this terror surely had human form. Cray's desperate need for company informed that easily, where a blaze of camaraderie had ganged up on the truth.

"A decade with your mates at sea and you'd be a lonely landlubber too." Those had been early words.

Back in the present moment, and Cray was not keen to leave the Paragon.

"The weather's good for a short hike," I suggested.

It took words from the proprietor for Cray to change his mind:

"The walk to Bridal Veil Falls is very popular." The security blanket he needed.

But down in the valley we didn't see anyone. Only mossy, dark tree ferns in primal clusters about the trail. Then Cray threw his arms up when a yellow-tailed black cockatoo circled up from the valley floor. Frightened by the blunt shriek, he was reassured by the cacophany as a flock of mountain lowrys swept over the blue gums. Crimson deception.

We had taken the cliff walk, one which hugs the smooth, dark mouth of a cave and where the frozen night had left a line of ice stalactites hanging from the rock. The spears of ice were as tall as Cray and seemed to be waiting for the sun to warm and unhinge them in a burst of gravity. Even as we stood, rubbing up against damp ferns and sassafras, we watched a great skewer come crashing down, shards of ice scattering across the path.

For Cray the alarm bells were going off again and fear was spiking within.

"Get me out of here. We're gonna be trapped I know it."

I thought of the Hollywood remedy — a slap across the face to settle the hysteric, but then Cray started raving about the death in the family.

"Louie and Joe, left out on the bridge. We thought they'd come down the hatch but we left them out to drown."

Cray's face looked swelled and pulsed a shade of blue in the green suffocating ocean of forest. Another skewer of ice came tumbling from the crest and I thought of torpedoes and the element of surprise and how Cray's whole heart was breaking up like a turbine out of action.

"My mates are dead. My lover . . . "

My arms caught him up as I shared in the tale and recalled the tabloids of the time. A terrible mistake just off the Heads, two young sailors drowned through negligence. As for the gay component, I didn't remember any mention of that, and Cray too denied all of it later, as soon as we were back inside the Paragon and well away from that primordial zone. Maybe none of it was true. Cray just rambling and distorting the facts to satisfy his submariner's fancy. But it had me thinking about all the others, the mates and pals and buddies who died together and how the world would always alter the truth about our lives.

So here we are. Back at Josef's birthday picnic. Cray's big grin and affection rolling out of control on all the company. Meantime, Julia draws circles in the sand, a horoscope for Josef whose "beautiful man is well on his way". It gives him solace and I wish Cray could find the same. I think I'm the only one who understands his secrets of love and death. But if the facts of history won't show it, then you wouldn't read about it either. So I'll just stay here next to Cray, wait for the party guests to make off home and wonder if life really is a ship of fools.

SASHA SOLDATOW

Memento Mori

My eyelids I have closed to phantoms
But distant hopes
Disturb my heart at times.

[In memory of Rennie and Martin]

I am trying to remember what my father's cock looked like. It is a dim memory, coloured by fantasy and masturbation. And an aura of loss. He's dead. Decayed most completely by now. It makes me wonder what I should do with my body when I'm dead. Or, to be more precise, what I now direct should be done, for I will not be around to witness anything. There is no post death, only dust by burning or dirt by decay. I prefer the dirt. I always have preferred processes that lead to filth in comparison to efficient disposal. To my ears, there is no music to cremation. Burning of a body should end in a fantastic explosion, the bitterest end.

Summoned to return home urgently and acting against my better judgement, I travel back and forth from Sydney to Melbourne. It is always Andrew I ring to pick me up from Tullamarine airport. In these moods of comparative loneliness he makes me feel less neglected. I try not to abuse his generosity. On the few occasions that I do, he snaps at me, quite correctly, too. Though I have to add that he too is sometimes moody.

It is May in Melbourne. Andrew drives me along the freeway to stay in his one bedroom flat in South Yarra. He is wearing his dirty boots and gardening work clothes, having taken precious time off earning money to pick me up. The city looms in the distance. I take small loving looks at him when he's not watching me. I am in such a state that I cannot tell if these loving looks are returned, though we laugh as we tell each other stories about our respective mothers.

It is May both here and in Vitebsk. That's where my grandmother was born. My grandmother is now in Box Hill Hospital, in intensive care, a catheter in her urethra, a drip in her arm and an oxygen mask over her face. She is dying. It is her time.

She has prepared herself for this. Privately, eight years ago, she told me that she has prayed for thirty years for this death. Her spiritual crisis is well and truly over. This, now, is the physical crisis. Falling on her knees in my mother's spare bedroom for the past thirty mornings and thirty nights before her ancient silver icon, she has begged The Holy Virgin to help her die. Unfortunately, her body has never obeyed her religious beliefs. It is a separation of needs.

After a marriage at thirteen in the 1920's in Soviet Russia, she birthed four children in eight years. Only the first child died, her only boy, of meningitis. He was two years old. Then, after a secret silence of sixteen years which no-one will tell me about, her husband died. This is all I know of him. Not a soldier, he was incarcerated in a prison camp by the German invaders for three months. The cause of his death was *schwindsucht*, a form of consumption, as it was called then, but the dictionary also defines it as 'a wasting disease that eats away at you'.

You'd think by now, now that she wishes to die so badly, so desperately, that my grandmother would be granted this ultimate favour. But her body won't listen. Through a heart attack and the insistent deterioration of old age, her body keeps on working, beating, breathing, shitting, her hapless lips telling her three dark daughters off in the most degrading, vulgar language, words that bubble out from somewhere in her past.

"You wouldn't believe how nasty she can be," says one of her three daughters, the one who wiped up her shit and piss the first time anyone was aware that this disgrace would be her permanent final state.

"Why won't he let me die?" my grandmother says, secretly, to me, of God. Her religion helps her. It is God that has let her down. But her faith will never let her confront such insolence.

When I arrive at the hospital, I sit at her bedside. Her lungs are packed tight with fluid. My mother tells me that this is all natural, that this is a process that has to happen. I don't know who she is talking to, me or herself.

My family has warned me that my grandmother recognises no-one, that she is in a semi-lucid coma and going quickly. Yet, when she sees me, she attempts a smile, repeats my diminutive name, *Sashenka,* over and over through her oxygen mask, tries to talk of something loving for a couple of minutes. It is difficult for her to say anything through her missing dentures and the mask that keeps her breathing. After a while she moves her head to one side and falls into a half-dream sleep. It is both tiredness and dignity. I stroke her beautiful hair. Throughout her whole life, her hair has always been as soft as down. While I tender her, she turns to me and softly says, "That is the caress of my angel." Then closes her eyes and falls into a deep calm sleep.

"You always die alone," I said to her, the last time she was in hospital.

"Yes," she replied, her eyes looking past her soul. "That is as it should be." This conversation bruises me forever.

There is no ambivalence about my memories or the way I use them. That's why I can never call them correct. They're not historically accurate. But that does not impede their vividness, their colour. This is the knowledge that I carry, the truth I have learned which has taught me to recognise when people have to be left alone.

As I leave the hospital, never to return to see her alive again, I am reminded of my father. I see him naked in a bathroom, but it is a green tiled bathroom in Sydney where he has never stood, never been. He never went to Sydney. So the cock I see, the cock I witness in this edge of memory, is something else. However, I have to note the fact that it is definitely still my father's cock, not someone else's. I have taken it upon myself to reconstruct the shape, the colour, the object, the desire. The place is of no importance. This cock is his and no-one else's.

I was never fucked by my father. I tell you this quickly in case temptation brings these thoughts to your mind. I'm not interested in religion, in the subconscious or the archetype. Nor am I interested in psychoanalysis or shrinks, something a local unknown doctor tries to suggest to me when I go to him for a simple script for Valium, for a drug which I know and, at this moment, need badly. To blot out the present, some would say, but which actually acts to blot out old beginnings.

I have to break this writing here. A bit of light relief, a pull of my own cock on the bed. Not only one pull as it turns out, but many, each one a quickly fantasised rebellion to rid the body of anxiety which even the Valium cannot allay.

Let me tell you what happens when I write about sex, even in a time of grief. Thinking these thoughts and writing them down, I get sexed up. I stroke myself, touch my nipples as

I tap the keys of my word processor. To not get stiff would be unnatural, to my male mind anyway. Though, when I write of murder I do not feel a similar need.

Men find masturbation simple. The spurt of sperm like phlegm. Easy to cough up. The penis is mightier than the sword. Laugh with me as I ejaculate.

I was never touched up by my father, never raped. Love and respect. No sin. That was dad when he was clothed. Naked, I have made him something else. Something more beautiful, like a soft caress, the touch, in retrospect, of a lover.

This last statement is spoken as a joke, but be warned. This writing is also sacred. I am burying my grandmother and, through her, particles of myself, though some pieces, like viruses, stay hidden, ready to re-infect.

A traditional Russian Orthodox funeral is exhausting. An open casket is frighteningly final. I enter the church bearing my gift of two wild roses which I place with her body. They are white. Everything is white except for her lips, the brightest red lipstick I've ever seen, applied as if by a crazed surrealist. The morticians have done an excellent job, made her look fifty-five whereas she was almost eighty-seven. Without realising it, the gash they have created across her mouth makes her look angry, makes her look like she has proudly taken on all of the dislocation of this century.

At her funeral, wearing an inappropriately old-fashioned tie (Ben's), a fancy jacket (borrowed from Bruce) and proper shoes (borrowed from Nelson), suddenly I am transformed. I am now the male elder-head of the family. It is a role I slip into easily, almost naturally. It is a role I do not want and do not respect, but I perform it magically, not showing the regression in my mind.

I am twelve again. My father is shaving. He is naked. Looking at my reflection in the mirror, he speaks to me of science, of mathematics and the universe.

We talk, I look. I can remember nothing of his face, his arms, shoulders, back or legs. That is not surprising since, as I am twelve, he is already dead. What I do remember is a description of a dick in a pre-teens sex education booklet. "A penis is like a short hose that hangs between your father's legs." The next book, for the adolescent boy, tells you of erections, even pictures a man with one, in black silhouette. The picture is silly. It is a boy's erection, not a man's. My father's cock was thicker. I know, I sucked it later, alone in my bed, after he was dead.

There is a lot of residual bullshit when you try to

reconstruct the past, but fantasy surprisingly provides a certain and necessary corrective. Like a fever, it is calm, sincere and undemanding, but it can also take its toll.

A friend tells me, recalling when he was a child, of having a bath after gardening, him sitting in the bath, his father standing under the shower. He remembers his father's cock level with his face. My friend is not sure — he thinks he is ten, maybe twelve. Every man I have asked tells of their father's cock in that moment just before puberty. When a cock becomes something to look out for. When a cock becomes something different to, say, your nose.

I have a thesis. Boys remember their father's cocks only when they realise the importance that their own cocks assume as the primary experience and focus of their own changing bodies. I do not use the word *importance* loosely. Previous to this interest, and even after, I am certain that all of us boys have seen our father nude, but very few of us remember the dangling hose till then, and afterwards we look and see it with a knowing, calculated disinterest. We invent a distance.

Boys' first thoughts are of their mother. Is this true? I do not know. It is a speculation. Except that my younger brother cannot bring himself to kiss the corpse of his mother's mother and stands behind all the mourners, lost in his own grief at this next repetition of a series of further mortalities.

I touched my grandmother's cunt once. She was lying in the dark in her bedroom in the family home in Victoria Street, Camberwell, weeping inconsolably after a screaming and unfair, vicious family fight. The actual facts of the argument will always remain forgotten, but her burning tears, alone in her room, were for herself and the status she was losing on the announcement that my mother was to remarry. Her favourite son-in-law, my father, was truly and finally never to return. In the darkness I came to comfort her.

Orientating myself badly in the dark, I walked blindly to her bed and touched her soft hair gently till I realised I was touching her between her legs and that she was naked. Her bitterness was so great that she did not respond.

This is in no way written to explain the reasons why I am gay. I was already thinking of men well before then. It is simply a statement of fact.

I am grateful that in Melbourne I have a man I love, a man I can stay with so that I can escape the destructive intimacy of my family. My love for all of them is deep, but the depth is harrowing.

Imagine me in Melbourne, staying with Andrew and

Nelson, his new lover. Imagine me masturbating my anxiety away over and over in the spare bed that Andrew always makes up for me. Imagine having adolescent feelings about my father at the age of forty-three in this death crisis. Imagine these two men whom I love, putting up with my undignified, brooding boring presence. Then flying home from Melbourne and having crying eyes, dead eyes. And that wrenched-out feeling of having just lost a father thirty years ago. And soon another death.

At home in Sydney I sleep on drugs for fifteen hours.

A friend the next day says I look rested, says I look wonderfully well. I smile with her and understand that she too is aging. It's not that the years start to rush by more quickly — its more that the last years of my life, be they five or forty, demand more intensity, less wasting of time, more companions, more intimacy, less people. More me and you and your lover and maybe a few other friends. You see, the youthful cry for help has evaporated, but the infant cry still persists.

After the death, when I return to Melbourne, I look at my mother at her own mother's funeral, standing by the casket with her two sisters, each one holding fast to a sensible black handbag. Later, after the event, the burial in the hole, I half-dream in Andrew's spare bed in the morning as Nelson kisses me as he leaves for work, and again later, in full daylight, as Andrew kisses me and leaves. I dream of my mother lying dead in her casket, and the only image is of some future memory, of her lying lifeless and of me passionately kissing her breasts.

I have not forgotten how much I need to talk with people about life. About its vicissitudes. How much I need to stay up late and chatter. Cry sometimes when I'm alone and, if I can't help myself, listen to recordings which sing of agony. It is a variant on sleeping with a man, you and you, and another you, though you might all turn into images of my father if I let you, because I am older than all of you.

There is a sexuality to death which is never discussed. I mention this in passing and won't elaborate because I am tired now from writing. My eyes hurt at the edges. They've got grit in them. Bits of shell. The sands of time.

It was nine years ago that I immediately fell in love with Andrew when I saw him at a party. One look, one conversation, one laugh. Obviously at first it was sexual, the feeling in my cock for a fuck. But our bodies did not connect correctly — you know these responses immediately though your ego will never let you acknowledge this, especially not in bed after trying. Even though we went to sleep tightly together after both coming off, we woke up apart. I do not know which of us has allowed our relationship to expand for this extent of time. For me it is a mutual love, but I can only speak of myself. Then I arrive in Melbourne and he introduces me to his lover and I fall hopelessly in love again.

The love of another look, too quick, too fast, caused this while I was sitting next to you in your car. Nelson, my fast new friend, the lights changed to green too quickly to kiss you. And I suddenly knew I had to leave this city immediately because if I stayed any longer I would ask you for a fuck and you would say no and the question and the answer would ruin everything for everyone.

I am not taking any risk in writing this. I have told this to both Andrew and Nelson. They will make of it as they will while I sit in Sydney and churn my heart out into a hundred drunken nights.

All my writing is an act of love. Some of it is specific, some less generous. Nelson, I once wrote my love out on paper for Andrew. I have also written it out for others. Never for my father. This is the first mention of him.

Writing about life is writing out a series of loving frustrations punctured through with heart-breaking longings. We attempt to delay these crises by eating and drinking with our friends. Making our talk an abandonment, an infinite enjoyment, which is ultimately the secret decay of hurt.

With some friends we also talk about life, try to unravel the conundrum, discover the obvious. Sometimes, while laughing heartily, I also hear myself hesitantly whispering as well. I listen to other's experiences, enjoin in a communion of deep conclusions about ourselves. But more often we unabatedly chatter, enjoy the arguments, the consolations. Then suddenly, usually when drunk, when the shark has mauled us and dragged us to the depths, we stagger into a battered silence about the things we cannot tell, about people we love and their deaths, things that are not proper talk.

With some few friends, though, and you have become one of these, we leave nothing to the imagination, no thought to chance. Then, after we have talked these life talks, searched and wrung out our souls, we part with each other to a taxi somewhere or, staying with you both, to a bed in the next room, the room away from where both of you sleep and fuck with one another. Hardly ever do true friends remain together afterwards. We always recognise when the time has come for the last embrace of the night.

There's a cute guy I remember while doing the beat in a

40

toilet in Marrickville probably twelve years ago. I remember because he couldn't get his cock stiff.

"Fuck," he says. I play with his dick but nothing happens. It's the hose from my youth but I'm older now and insane for action.

"Sorry," he says, as another man enters. I suck this new man's cock. It's a nondescript engagement. Finally he pulls his cock out of my mouth and lifts me up, turns me around to fuck me. Anything, I'll do anything. I spread my legs, offer my bum, bend my legs a bit to make his entry easier.

There are three of us. Me, the man behind me fucking my arse, and the guy I like. He stands there hoping the sight and smell of buggery will turn him on. The guy behind me is doing his job — it's pleasant enough, but it's more like a wank than a fuck. I'm a hole, that's enough for him. I don't mind. For a moment I am a compliant partner.

The man with the limp dick, my no-action friend, as I decide to think of him, watches me being fucked, not knowing whether to go or stay.

"Play with my nipples," I say quietly to this lost soul, as I arch my back so that the man behind can finish his business.

After the cock shoving is all over and the man has come and gone, as it were, zipping his pants up, I kiss my half-neglected friend gently on the lips.

"Do you live with anyone?" he asks.

"No-one," I reply, his tongue kissing me.

I cannot remember any detail of the night we spent together. Nothing. My diary entry for that day reads, 'Ring Phillip re tape.' And then, enigmatically in pencil, 'I'll wipe your tears.' I never see him again.

It doesn't puzzle me, but it intrigues me a little, these boy-friends that I have accumulated that I can ring up after midnight. Friends I can talk to about my father's cock. Friends who will pick me up at the airport in a moment of crisis. Friends who will open a bottle of wine for me when I arrive and who will wipe away my tears with harsh but accurate words of truth that make us both laugh.

As my tears well in my eyes and I wipe them quickly away because I do not really want to cry, you pour me another drink and tell me I'm drinking far too much. Then you make me a sandwich because I am not hungry anymore. Eat it, you say. I obey.

Alone in my single bed, after you have both left me, I have a recurring fantasy. I am walking somewhere in the snow. It is getting dark and I am lost. I am also running a fever. There is a solitary house in the distance. Lights shine through the windows like bright stars on a moonless night. I approach, knock on the door. It is opened by a man and I am hit from all directions by warmth and coldness at the same time. Without a word, he takes me in. Feels my brow. Then carefully puts me to bed.

When I wake, I do not know how many centuries have passed, but I am over the worst. Looking around, I see him by my side. He smiles and makes me some tea, sits with me as I drink it. The tea has lemon and sugar, just as I like it.

"You should get up. I'll help you have a shower," he says, tentatively touching me. "It'll help you feel better." Then adds, "Don't be embarrassed about being naked. After all, I did have to undress you, so there's nothing I haven't seen."

As I get out of bed, he hands me a towel and touches me again. It is the touch of kindness. After I have washed myself, I stand before him like an unprotected newborn child. He hugs me, like a lover, then wipes my body dry of the tears of generations.

This piece of writing is for the many of you, my new and aging boys, one of whom I call my dad.

MARK TRY

Desire As

Once, when Jump brought a squaw to one of Auntie
Gertie's parties, my mother said, 'he just does it'. She said it in
the same tone she used when my father banged every
cupboard door in the kitchen at six in the morning when he had
dawn shifts — 'he just *does* it' — or when one or the other of
us didn't replace the toilet roll, or our underpants. (Well I don't
see why I should incriminate myself unnecessarily: it was only
Ned and Alistair who wore their underpants for three days
running, never me. And I don't think Sam ever wore any). So I
suppose that when she said it about Jump, the rest of the
sentence was supposed to be the same unspoken accusation
we recognised when she said it about any of us: 'to annoy me.'
We just did it to annoy her. As if, when I sat on the bog and the
last tissues of Sorbent came off in my hand, I grinned malic-
iously to myself and thought, 'I'll fix that bitch ; I just *won't*
replace the toilet roll' (laughs devilishly). As if, when Jump
went to Canada to study, he thought to himself, 'Now, what can
I do that would really piss Stella off . . . ' And it had come to him
in an instant of brilliant illumination, 'Of course! I'll take a
squaw back home.'

My mother stood gawking (squawking) in the pantry at
Belle's place that night, I remember, and said, 'Jesus' a lot to
Belle's back. It wasn't just that she was busy putting passion-
fruit on the pavlova; Belle was genuinely one of those people
who never let anything bother her. At least that's how she was
by the time I really got to know her. Along the way I'd picked
up fragments of her life from my mother letting things drop; I
mean, I knew that she'd been married three times, and I even
had vague recollections of her last two husbands who I'd never
called uncle because they came in such quick succession. And
I knew that she couldn't have children, although I didn't find
out why until I was sixteen and the revelatory story of her
abortion with a wire coat-hanger when she was fifteen crossed

my mother's lips in tones that said, 'And now that you're old enough I'll tell you, but don't tell Lucy or Sam' (because, I now know, she wanted to tell them herself when they reached my age — I told them anyway). So Belle came in for reassessment then: it was less that she never let anything bother her, than that she had ceased to be able to be bothered. Of course, at twelve, at Auntie Gertie's party, it seemed to me quite simply that I would rather have had Belle for my mother than my mother. Childless aunties always have that attraction, I now realise. Actually, Ned's kids think the same of me as an uncle, or so his wife tells me. I'm not sure that I ever thought it of Jump. Well, for one thing he was never around long enough for me to form an opinion about anything to do with him. He had a flat at Bondi that I can vaguely remember visiting one day when I was about seven, and my mother and father arguing about going there all the way in the car (neither of them wanted to but they both felt uncomfortably obliged, I think). And then he was hardly ever in Sydney. He studied in Melbourne for three years and then at Oxford for another two before he came home when Grandpa died and hung around for about six months ('waiting to see how much the old bugger's left him, that's why,' said my father). Originally he went to Canada to study again, but he got a tenured position at — of all places, I now think ironically — Queen's University. Where he met the squaw. Her name was Imogen, and I said it over and over again to myself for a week because I thought it was such a beautiful name. She had the broadest Canadian accent I had ever heard — well I hadn't heard that many, I suppose, and maybe it's just that it seems so strange in retrospect — and she wore dresses with white tassles around the hem and nothing in the front so that her tits nearly fell out. She didn't have very big tits; in fact, she was pretty thin, which is how my father came to continually refer to her as Cher, I think. Well, the thinness, the black hair, those dresses. And she had a huge mouth full of wonderful white teeth. I remember that one day when my mother took me to the dentist about a month after Gertie's party, the dentist explained in great detail (with motions) how I should brush and I looked at my mother and said that I'd love to have teeth like Imogen. I'll never forget the look on her face.

I like to think now that Jump loved her name and her teeth too. I should have said that the other reason I never thought of him as a particularly interesting rel, like I thought of Belle, was because — to completely contradict myself — I sort of agreed with my mother in a way and believed that he really *did* 'just do it' to annoy her. I guess I still do, although now I feel no more interest in him than I did then, just a curious sorrow — for both of us, I think. My mother basically would have preferred it if he had just conformed to her pattern of niche-ifying everyone and made up his mind whether he really wanted to sleep with men or women, instead of going from one to the other all the time. This, of course, never occurred to me at the time. Christ, I was only twelve — and even then, I had the sexual knowledge of a six year old. I had no idea that David — who shared the flat with Jump at Bondi — was his lover. It didn't even occur to me when David sat me on the end of the double bed in the only bedroom in the place and bounced me so that I could feel the water rippling under my hands and bum and held my knee. Why should it have? At that time, I was only seven, and my only other remotely sexual experiences between then and when I was twelve were when Lucy pulled down her pants in the backyard one day when we were having a fight — not to tease me, but as an insult (I'd once pulled mine out and sort of flung it in her direction while I stuck my tongue out and told her to nick off) — and when Alistair and I had stood at the loo basin together and peed in from opposite sides, all the time discussing the way our skin had been sewn in different ways. We both became hard, but now he's as straight as an arrow with twins and another one on the way, so I guess that never counted for anything. I'd never conceived of desire as anything that might be so consciously aroused and pointed until I decided I wanted my hands around Imogen's little tits and to thumb the nipples. And she let me. I never told anyone — never have. I wonder if she ever told Jump. A tiny part of my regret about not knowing him better was that I never got to ask him.

At his funeral I met two of his lovers for the first time. Neither Imogen nor David were there, but these two had known Jump when he lived at Oxford, and now they live out here. Alex has AIDS, too. He looks okay, although my mother reckons he looks like 'death warmed up', but then that's her way of having a go at me again. She loves me terribly, so much I'm still embarrassed by the things she says to me. It's taken me all these years to realise that she loved Jump in almost exactly the same way. He was the little brother of five girls, and all the big sisters were there around the grave to throw dirt on him. I threw some too and watched Alex watching the lowering box. I know it's silly, well it ought to be anyway, but I'm sure that part of Alex's reason for coming to the funeral was just to annoy my mother. I have this curious conviction that when Alex was at Jump's bedside in the weeks before he died, the pair of them connived and contrived it together. Suzie is the other lover from Oxford; I can see Jump grabbing tightly onto Alex's hand in the hospital room and saying, 'You and Suzie've got to stand together opposite Stell, that'll get her going.' And of course it did. She muttered something about desire as inexplicably fickle, as we went back to the car from the graveside, and I was delighted that something so simple should confound her sense of surety so easily. Well, not delighted — that sounds malicious, doesn't it? — just amused, maybe. I know it's not the same thing, and it's hardly comparable, but she can so easily rationalise and accept the courage to remove an unwanted child with a wire coathanger, and yet not even begin to understand the courage needed to live your life outside what even I'd call 'what's normal'. I wonder if she would have understood Belle's decision if she had decided — or been allowed to decide — to keep her child. I think I make her a little easier because I've got Ben and I'm not leaping in and out of bed with other men, not to mention women. I'm comfortably (comfortingly) categorised. Although I still grin and agonise over her reaction when I first told her about my desire for men rather than women. She just sat stiff at the dining room table, folded her fingers together, and said to me so bloody earnestly: 'But why ?'

IAN MacNEILL

Tiberius' Funeral

Tiberius wanted to know if he could be cremated in a cardboard box, so he rang Rationale Funerals.

Then he relented and decided the scientists might as well get some use out of his organs, if no-one else could.

He'd got cross with his Ankali person and the social worker and decided if you wanted something done properly you'd better go ahead and do it yourself. So he was doing his funeral.

"Look, here's the money. Go down to the shop and buy the Mirror," he'd said to the Ankali person on her second visit, "give us something to get disgusted about," when she'd tried getting spiritual again. She wasn't a bad sort, old Lorraine, had a bit of a sense of humour, so he'd keep her on, he'd decided after the month's probation he'd given her.

He found it necessary to murmur to the social worker, "If you're not a bit more direct I might appoint you executor of my whole bloody Carlton Ware collection. Why don't you just come out and say, have you made a will yet. And yes, I have. It's with The Public Trustee — he, or she is my executor. But Tim, like hair, believe me, that can be changed. Just think of all those little orphaned plates and dishes you might have on your conscience. Let me see . . . I left the water lily to Lily and nobody's seen her since she took off with . . . oh well, never you mind . . . but remember some things are better left unsaid." And he'd sighed. By this time Tim had unlearned enough not to say, "You seem a bit tired."

Tiberius made it to the phone to ring the rector of a conveniently situated church, the congregation of which had once given one of his friends who was it's organist some trouble when he came out. He inquired about renting the hall and the facilities for tea-making. Then he rang the friend of a friend who was trying to get something going in catering and invited him in for a bit of a chat. He spent a week on the list of names.

Several were added and subtracted more than twice as Tibi weighed and balanced, forgave and found he could not forget.

On the whole, he was magnanimous.

He asked one last favour of a music queen friend — would he please, before doing whatever with the records, just record these selections for — what? One could hardly describe Callas singing — well anything — 'background', but just four tapes worth of . . . and he handed him the list of selections. Three had to be done again and then one side each of two, then, just to get it right, Nina Simone singing . . . and the Etude needs more volume.

He was called Tiberius because the name came with him from the primordial days, because he looked rather like a large gingery cat and because he seemed hilariously like the type one thought the emperor was. Though some people, on certain occasions, had had occasion to say, "*Now* I know why you're called Tiberius."

For example, people thought and some said amongst themselves, after a drink or two, "He'd be gorgeous if he worked out in a gym," but one foolish creature, momentarily dazzled with a sense of his own success in the matters of gyms, actually said to Tibi, "You ought to join a gym, work on your definition."

Tibi regarded him. "I suppose gyms are useful for health purposes," he finally said, softly, "but they're not the sort of place I would care to be seen hanging about. And isn't there something about the expense of spirit on a waist?"

The memorial afternoon tea began on time when the caterers tore the gladwrap off the trays of sandwiches and opened the first bottle of champagne at four o'clock, as arranged. The tea facilities were indeed used and there was orange juice and even mineral water (Tiberius had said, "I suppose we must, in case there's someone I can't think of right now who never got past it but two bottles will be a largesse, I hope."), cola ("for any children"), dark fruit cake and lamingtons.

People would stop their various conversations with the memories the tape selections brought, sometimes involving Tibi. The last one was the Stones' *Ruby Tuesday* and those who could, heard Tibi's voice saying:

"Forgive the indulgence of that.

I know it's your funeral too.

Did the champagne hold out?"

GARY DUNNE

A Midnight Shift

Inside the nightclub it's hot. The Kiwi cloakroom clerk flirts, claiming to be a film-maker. Simon decides it's a pleasant change from unemployable fashion designer, an ex-Auckland cliche around innovative Darlo. He leaves his jacket and pushes through the crowd.

In the usual corner, Mike, in ragged denim, all fringes artificially bleached, looks bored.
"You're late," he pronounces. "And tonight's dead."
"No one interested, hey?"
"Nothing fuckable. Prehistoric clones. Hens dressed up as chicken. And fucking yuppies," gesturing at a pair of post-Country Road college boys, "Probably from Melbourne."
"Bigot."

Simon doesn't stay. He's spotted Glen, the seduction of whom, over a number of weeks, is turning into a surprisingly enjoyable soapie. Glen is next to the bar, pretty as a picture. Simon orders drinks. Glen says he's well. So is Simon. There's this predictable pattern to the conversation. Simon runs through some of the things they have in common, paying particular attention to Glen's sixties sensibilities. Glen replies, adds a bit here and there, smiles when flattered and shows interest.

When they first met, Simon casually invited him home to examine his prophylactic collection. "Not on the first date," was the reply and Simon at first thought he was joking. He wasn't. That seems like ages ago. Now things are cooler. THE BIG W says GLEN-BOY is a prick-teaser. Simon disagrees. He likes the measured responses, enough to keep him hanging on and a bit more. It's constant and that's OK.

They hit the dance floor. Much eye contact and limited but fluid movement. Nearby, a pair of gym queens with matching shorts and moustaches are sharing a bottle of amyl. Not such an anachronism given the music being played. Glen seems equally amused. Once upon a time there was a theory connecting amyl with AIDS. It always seemed to Simon that it only caused premature shirt removal.

Back at the bar, the conversation is unusually brief. Glen has to go. He wants to start work early tomorrow. His fascination with a computer's varied functions is one of the things they don't have in common. Simon suggests dinner one night. Glen likes the idea but won't be specific. He leaves, promising to ring during the coming week. Simon heads back to Mike.

"How is GLEN-BOY?"

"My favourite waste of time."

"No man is worth that much bother," replies Mike. All he can see is an inexplicable persistence, a lusting for the nearly impossible.

"It's not like that," says Simon, not sure how to put it into words.

"Just lay your cards on the table. 'I don't suppose a fuck would be out of the question.' Or something like that. Get things moving."

"I don't know. So far we've only moved things as far as the coffee shop over the road. He knows I'm keen. I'm not going to make a fool of myself. There are new rules. The next move is his."

"Or yours," says Mike, unconvinced.

Tall and imposing, in what looks like a polyester sari, THE BIG W, pushy transvestite glamour star, parts the crowd to join them carrying a round of drinks.

"Let's welcome our new contestant on Blankety Blanks," announces Simon, his best Graham Kennedy impersonation, "THE BIG W herself, Miss Margaret Whitlam."

Mike claps.

THE BIG W bows, then sits, beaming. No-one's done this number in ages and it's her favourite piece of seventies baggage.

"Tell us the Margaret Whitlam story," continues Simon.

"Well Graham. I'm over 21. I live in Darlinghurst. I like meeting men."

"Triple tragedy," mutters Mike.

"A or B Margaret?"

"I'll take B, GRA-GRA."

"You always take B," says Mike.

"A limited range of options."

"Maybe we should try something more up to date one night. For a change. Like Perfect Match. They do Perfect Match in Newtown."

"Nothing they do in Newtown surprises me anymore. . . I don't care if it dates me. I am what I am. And anyway, I don't like Perfect Match. The contestants overact."

They settle back to dish. Dishing is an American word Mike picked up from Tom. It means bitching. And in L.A., bitching means something else again. In the current climate it's less likely Mike will sleep with an American and thus get a chance to show off his knowledge of their lexicon. Still, he keeps it filed with the details on Willard's toupée, the chance may yet arise.

After a couple of rounds of drinks, Mike begins to look flat.

"My life," his voice slurs," is in Tupperware containers. Work. Sex. Health. Here. The pub. All separate."

He's Simon's best friend, but once he's on to talking neurotic, he's like a cracked record.

"All separate. The problem is keeping it together. Making connections. Otherwise it's all too fragmented."

Simon says nothing. He's known Mike too long. Obsessions aren't changed by well meant advice. His optimism, from talking with Glen, is fading.

"I mean dealing with things. Like Scott being positive. It worries me."

"Probably worries him too," says THE BIG W, filing her nails. A bad sign.

Simon tries to remember who Scott is and wonders if he slept with him.

"You have to keep the lid on. Like it might all explode or something."

"I didn't know you were such good friends with those Double Bay socialites," says THE BIG W.

Simon places Scott. An aerobic airhead. Not his type at all.

"Tom told me. He knows them better than I do. After he rang me I couldn't sleep. I went walking. At four am. Walked miles. There was this storm. Thunder, lightning, wind. Real drama queen stuff. Anyway, near Ultimo, I stopped, looked around and thought, 'Shit. A girl could get mugged out here.' So I got a taxi back home."

"You should have stayed home, popped two valium and taken a bubble bath. That's what I do on those kind of nights." THE BIG W has never believed in leaving emotions churning around in a blender.

"Did you get off with him?" asks Simon.

"I'm not sure . . . I don't know . . . It's the big picture . . . Back rooms. But we don't do that anymore, do we Simon? We get here on time . . . And we sit and we put lids on it. Tupperware lids . . . Not much else to do . . . My life in Tupperware . . . "

"Try wanking," suggests Simon sharply. "But not in the bubble bath. The cum goes all stringy."

"Or a pick-up. Just insist on a love-glove if you're worried about them getting too deep and meaningful." THE BIG W gestures at the bar line-up. "There's plenty to choose from. You could get lucky. At this late hour they ain't so fussy."

"Safe sex or a wank," Mike slurs, unimpressed.

"I'd take B," says Simon. "A looks awfully jaded tonight." He nods at the closing rush of stressed denim.

"So does THE PHARMACEUTICAL KID," says THE BIG W as Mike's head gently lands on the table.

"I'll walk him home," Simon finishes Mike's drink.

"It's OK. I will. It's on my way."

"Did you two end up going for tests?" asks THE BIG W as they reach the street. Mike shows signs of reviving in the cold, fresh air. He spews in the gutter.

"I'm going. Mike's not sure. CLEOPATRA, the queen of denial. Reckons she's neurotic enough already."

"I'm like you. I'd rather know."

"I'd rather know as long as it is negative."

DENIS GALLAGHER

Sebastian, Dinosaur

Sebastian is dressed in leather harness, jeans with exposed bandana in back pocket, key chain with keys, and boots. T-shirt optional. He enters, exuding machismo. Lingering pause as he displays himself centre stage.

[Gushes] Hi, everybody. Just thought I'd drop by. It's me, Sebastian. I met you all here on this very spot, a year ago. Remember? If you didn't catch me then . . . anyway, you remember me — Sebastian, Mister Sydney Buns, 1976!
Pregnant pause

[Humbled] It's not your fault if you've forgotten me, really. I must confess my profile has dropped a lot over the last twelve months, and I know I'm not pulling my weight like I used to. Yes, it's early nights now. But, let's face it, there isn't anywhere left to go anymore . . . except here at the fabulous Shift. The past is still alive and living here.
Moves to wall and embraces it:
These walls, O these walls . . . How I remember . . . years ago . . . when they used to be painted black and the sweat poured down them on those hot Saturday nights when the place was so packed not even the licensing squad could get in.

Over there . . . that's where Rabbit used to bop up and down like a pygmy . . . and over there . . . that's where Maroon T-shirt used to dance like he was falling off his surfboard . . . and Streak . . . and the Degro Twins . . . where have they all gone? The leather queens, where are they all now? Give it another few years and they'll be searching for us like some extinct species. I'll still be around. I'll be able to tell them *everything* — about those late night sessions at the Barracks, The Signal and Club 80. They can count on me. I've saved a tin of Crisco to prove it. And some of those coloured bandanas, and a key chain, and a pair of 501's, and a solid silver nail file. I'm into history.

How time flies, how things do change. Yes I'm quieter now . . . but not all that quiet . . .

[Overjoyed] MARDI GRAS! MARDI GRAS! MARDI GRAS!

It's that time of year again when all the true party queens like me get to go to heaven again. It's my busiest time. I've just traded in the Husqvarna on a brand-new Pfaff. My dears, does it *cook*. Anyway . . . I know everyone's just dying to know what I'm going to get up to after last year's effort. Well, that's why I've dropped by, specially, to share a secret or two with you and give away a little advice about the parade and you. This is the voice of experience speaking.

Tip number one. I've been in enough parades to know the only place to go is *up* . . . and . . . *big is best* — the bigger the better for everyone to see you — do them a favour. Mark my words, that's an important lesson to be learned in this bustlin' town. Of course, I practice what I preach, so this year I'm going to be bigger and better than ever. Wait for it. I'm going as a dinosaur — a twenty-foot-high dinosaur. And that's not all — I'm going to be on a leash (that's the leather bit) which is going to be held once again by my dear Betty. She's going as a prawn, we think — a big prawn . . . walking upright on two legs just like me. Yes, we're into nature . . . with improvements. Betty's got it into her head she's not going to be outdone by me, so she's going as a blinding pink ultra-violet prawn. Poor Betty . . . she doesn't know it but fashion has passed her by — BRIGHT IS OUT. That's tip number two. Fashion reflects the times we live in and these are troubled times, let me tell you. Colours are going back to safe, understated tones. That is why my dinosaur is *beige*. Betty says dinosaurs died out because they were beige, but what does she know? We all know where she belongs — throw another queen on the barbie!

Big and beige, that's going to be me. That prize is going to be mine, at last, after years and years . . .

[Recovering] We've been working on our costumes in Betty's back garden in Paddington. It's so tiny, like all of them — another good reason to build up not out.

I know she is going to kill me for telling, but here goes. The truth is, Betty hasn't yet decided yet whether it's going to be the prawn or the platypus . . . another last minute decision for Betty . . . she thrives on dilemmas . . . what used to be known as a drama queen. Last year she couldn't decide whether she was going to be an angel or a big toe. She went as the toe — more like her true self — with hairs on it and, of course, the nail was painted pink and, of course, it rained and Betty's big toe turned into a hairy pink mushroom somewhere between Taylor Square and the Showground. That's why this time it's the prawn or the purple platypus for her — they're both waterproof. But she's still got her colours wrong.

This year, no drugs. Just a daiquiri or two. We've invented one specially for the night . . . it's called Primeval Slime. That should give us a head start on everyone. That's a sort of tip.

Getting to the Parade can be a problem . . . there's no taxi big enough. A positive attitude is the solution. Let the Parade come to you. The moment you step onto the street, that's when it starts. And that's tip number three-and-a-half for everyone.

Anyway, I don't want to stop the show. I've bared my soul enough, but it's all for a good cause — education. Remember BIG IS BEST, BRIGHT IS NOT, and . . . LET THE PARADE COME TO YOU.

[Threatening] But don't underestimate me. I won't be taken advantage of! If I see another dinosaur in the Parade I swear I will turn Oxford Street into a bloodbath. Don't you dare get in my way, any of you. It's going to be all mine . . . this year I just know I'm going to blow the bum right out of the Best Costume Award.

See you at the Parade, I know you'll see me . . .

This monologue was first performed at the Midnight Shift, Sydney, in February 1986 as part of the cabaret, *Love, Sex and Romance*.

GILES HUGO

Hendrik Gatbek - Electro Autofellationist

The rise and ultimate detumescence of Professor Hendrik Gatbek should serve as a cautionary tale for the nineties. It should convince sexual pioneers and innovators that enough is as good as an orgy and there are, indeed, limits to erotic excess.

Before his demise, Gatbek was rich, famous and envied. His reputation as the most eminent sage in his own chosen sphere could not have been more brilliant; his books and monographs on sexual anthropology were acclaimed by everyone from Margaret Mead and Masters and Johnson to Germaine Greer and William Burroughs. His coffee-table glossy, *Safe Sex in 80 Ways Around the World*, had sold 12 million copies — 7 million in the USA alone — and had been translated into 25 languages, including Swahili, Cantonese, Semiotese, Urdu, Esperanto and braille. He had become the darling of deviant yuppies from Beverly Hills to Balmain. His speaking tours, which included live demonstrations by his multi-ethnic research assistants, were booked out months in advance. He was even asked to lecture in Moscow when glasnost finally penetrated the socio-sexual Iron Curtain. His video series *The G-Spot Ain't All You've Got* stayed on top of the sales and rental charts for two years and was banned in Iran, Iraq, Fiji, South Africa, Turkey, and Tasmania. It was even discussed by the Vatican Council and the Jewish Boards of Deputies in 17 countries.

Hendrik was hot. He had it all — and then some — so what went wrong?

Of course, the tabloids ran a totally fanciful rumour about a transsexual albino dwarf, who was allegedly seen leaving his apartment late on the night of his death, and there were risque allusions to deviant sexual practices and a peculiar form of electronic apparatus which might have contributed to his end, but in fact they didn't know the half of it.

I know, I was there, I saw it all.

You see, it was I who tenderly bid his remains adieu, fed the electric eels in the breeding tank and let myself out, after pausing to pocket his diary, his notes, the video tapes, and his mysterious little black book. Naturally, I alerted his lawyer and the police the next morning — after a suitable interval, during which I was able to establish an alibi with the metropolis's best-connected madam. Not that I suffered any guilt, though I may have put a few of my speculative, half-baked ideas into his eclectic head — ideas which had fertilised his own aberrant concepts, germinated, developed and matured into a fatal obsession: the ultimate orgasm.

Like many men of genius, Hendrik had humble origins which might have stifled his greatness had it not been for a series of chance meetings in his formative years. The only child of a Dutch immigrant couple who had arrived with nothing and set up a successful plumbing business in a small outback town after the war, Hendrik was quiet and studious. Nobody suspected then that this frail, tow-headed teenager, with a slight squint to his pale blue eyes and a stammer mixed in with his guttural accent, would one day be feted as a pathfinder in the field of sexual anthropology — and denigrated as a demon of sensual depravity.

It did not take him long to begin informal research, gathering his data by a novel but practical method. Although he went to school every weekday, he spent many of his weekends and all his vacations as a plumber's mate with his dad, repairing pipes, installing hotwater geysers, unblocking drains and sewers, and sorting out problems in septic tanks. He began making mental notes about what they discovered discarded in the sewage and relating these finds to the cultural and religious practices and pretensions of the residents of the homes they visited.

Crucifixes on the walls of every room in a home and a shrine to the Virgin were no guarantee that they wouldn't find used condoms and perhaps a discarded diaphragm among the detritus blocking a sewer pipe. He thought he had seen it all when the Reverend Percival Mucklethorpe's septic tank yielded up several items of women's undergarments and frilly negligees, and although Reverend Mucklethorpe gave Hendrik's father an unasked for present of a bottle of scotch and a case of communion wine, in addition to his fee, it remained unclear whether the items of female apparel had belonged to a regular visitor to the manse, or if they had formed part of the reverend gentleman's own after-hours wear.

But the discovery which topped them all, and was to launch Hendrik Gatbek on his sexual and academic career, came from the blocked sewer at Saint Virginia's College for Young Ladies. By then Henk had left school at the age of 15 to become a reluctant, but uncomplaining apprentice plumber, working for his father. He was doing a job at St Virginia's on his own, since his father was otherwise engaged that day. After he had finished the work and cleaned himself, he asked to see the headmistress, Miss Edna Stone, to advise her about how to prevent a recurrence of the blockage. The interview, which was conducted behind the closed door of Miss Stone's private study, lasted 45 minutes, at the end of which Hendrik emerged with a smile like the cat who had eaten the cream, and Miss Stone's normally wan pallor had been replaced by a veritable glow of dreamy satisfaction. In his bag of tools Hendrik took with him the cause of the sewer blockage — a miscarried foetus of about 10 weeks.

In exchange for promising to dispose of the sorry evidence and preserve the reputation of St Virginia's, Hendrik had enjoyed the first of many languorous interludes on Miss Stone's chaise longue. In return Miss Stone, who was not as virginal as her reputation or her nickname of The Ice Maiden suggested, was given the honour and pleasure of discovering that the otherwise unexceptional-looking young plumber's apprentice was extremely well-endowed — a length of eight inches flaccid and ten erect; a diameter four inches flaccid and five and a half erect. In the next couple of months he was called back at least a dozen times to St Virginia's to fix leaks, adjust ballcocks, lag pipes and install a bidet in Miss Stone's bathroom.

It was also Miss Stone who first interested Hendrik in anthropology — she had a master's degree and he consumed everything she had in her private library, which was fairly extensive. Hendrik was a sharp lad, so two years later, when he was called upon to unblock a drain at the Convent of the Immaculate Conception, he went well prepared. A lifelike doll, suitably coated in pig's blood and filth and flashed for a few seconds before the Mother Superior's startled gaze, was enough to convince the worthy lady that a few minutes of mortal sin was a fair exchange for preserving the convent's reputation — and her job. Hendrik was only nominally a Protestant, so his conscience was not terribly burdened by duping a Catholic. However the impact he — and of course his spectacular appendage — made on the Mother Superior was so devastating that after a deep, but brief, struggle with her convictions, she renounced her vows and left the order to become again simply Sarah Smith — and she shacked up with the young plumber.

They both had to leave town, so they headed for Sydney, where Hendrik worked to support his new bosom companion in a cupboard-like apartment. They also co-authored *Sexuality and Silence in the Cloisters: Lesbianism and Masturbation in a Closed Religious Community*. No publisher would touch it, so they printed it privately and quickly distributed 500 copies — mostly through porn bookshops — until its true scientific value was recognised in the academic community and it was quickly snapped up by an international publisher for reprints and translation into nine languages.

Their next book, *The Myth of Chastity: Abortion and Childbirth in Catholic Convents* earned them the enmity of the Vatican, thousands of dollars, and honorary doctorates from a couple of the more progressive universities in the US, Europe and Australia. At this point, they parted amicably; she became a feminist celebrity in her own right, while Hendrik took up a research post at Sydney University. It was there that I met him and impressed him with by first-hand research methods for my thesis, *The Drover's "Wife": Bestiality in Outback Australia*. When the university refused to grant me a doctorate, Gatbek resigned in protest and took me on as his chief research assistant for a hazardous, but exciting, field trip to the Middle East, which resulted in several syphilis treatments for both of us and two books, *Sodomy and Sand: Khawal Prostitutes in Egypt* and *One Hump or Two: The Camel as Sex Fetish*. This earned Gatbek an honorary doctorate from Tel Aviv University — and death threats from the PLO and the Ayatollah. Nothing seemed too sacred or hazardous for this precocious son of a Dutch immigrant plumber. After infiltrating a Trappist monastery in Sardinia to research *The Bulging Cassock: Sign Language and Seduction in a "Celibate" All-Male Community*, he entered South Africa on a false passport — if he had used his own he undoubtedly would have been detained immediately as all his books were banned by the Pretoria government — where he did research for *The Black Madonna: Miscegenation and the Myth of Afrikaner Racial Purity*.

It was then that we embarked on our most demanding and time-consuming project to date — five years in the Amazon headwaters to produce a film, *Human Sacrifice and Cannibalism in Primitive Amazonian Fertility Rites*, a documentary so gruesomely spectacular and sexually explicit that after its first showing at a conference in Amsterdam, copies of the film were seized by the vice squad and several of Gatbek's honorary degrees were withdrawn. It mattered little to Prof Gatbek; he had progressed way beyond the objective and scientific limitations of the ivory tower.

It was also on this trip that I discovered and introduced him to the bizarre ritual masturbation technique of the medicine men among the Otasama Indians. The practitioner first caught an electric eel in a bark-fibre net and exhausted most of its charge by touching its electrode-like tail to a series of live guinea pigs. When the discharge merely stunned the animal instead of killing it, the medicine man stuffed the eel's head up his anus to rest against the prostate gland and then touched the eel's electrode-like tail to the middle of his forehead — the position of the legendary "Third Eye". The orgasmic convulsions could kill a weak man — I saw it happen — and the eel's state of charge had to be carefully gauged to prevent ecstatic electrocution.

Nevertheless, we both tried it more than once, and I can assure you that even the 'all-orifices-meat-sandwich' ritual of the hermaphrodite Kirquaal tribes in Patagonia bears no comparison.

When we returned to Gatbek's Potts Point eyrie, we carried with us a dozen electric eels for research purposes. Gatbek didn't want to use them to repeat the experiment — that was too dangerous. Instead he carried out careful research with them to determine exactly what voltage and amperage was necessary to produce the required electrical discharge. Then he built a shock device with one electrode attached by a headband to the 'third eye' position, while the other took the form of a domed copper head on a ceramic dildo which could be inserted up the rectum to make contact with the nerve ganglia around the prostate gland. He dubbed the device the Orgazmatron.

The results were spectacular. Anyone who experienced one of Gatbek's electro orgasms was hooked, and normal sex was mundane by comparison. Gatbek was like a kid with a new toy. It was as if he had invented batteries and the vibrator all at the same moment. He also experimented with a female volunteer, Gertie de Smegma, his most trusted field worker, and discovered that the so-called female G-spot was equally effective as the point of internal contact. Gatbek swore us all to secrecy while he experimented with the potential of the Orgazmatron apparatus; he knew that there would be extreme resistance from the medical fraternity and the moral majority if he tried to publicise or market his device.

"Remember," he told us, "what the American Medical Association, the Food and Drug Administration and the FBI did to Wilhelm Reich and his theories about orgones and the orgone box. They hounded him to his grave. He may have been slightly off-beam, but he didn't deserve what they did to him. Poor old Wilhelm . . . I tell you, what we are working on is, in terms of sexual enjoyment, like the splitting of the atom in nuclear physics. It could do for sexual pleasure what the internal combustion engine did for transport — imagine, sexual nirvana without the risks of pregnancy, AIDS or other STDs."

He licked his lips and smiled. "Mine kinders, if we could refine the Orgazmatron and prove it safe, sexual intercourse between couples in advanced societies might become virtually obsolete, reserved entirely for procreation by those who want children. I mean, who is going to settle for sardines or tuna when he can dine on rainbow trout or caviar?"

He also started experimenting with multiple electrodes to stimulate various erogenous regions simultaneously. Eventually he devised a wiring harness for the Orgazmatron with additional optional electrodes on the nipples, the ear lobes, the glans of the penis (or the clitoris in women), and the tip of the tongue. By varying the amperage on each of these electrodes and pulsing the electrical discharge, Gatbek could 'tune' and prolong orgasm for several minutes — in fact until momentary unconsciousness ensued.

It was, unfortunately, I who made the chance comment which was to lead Gatbek to his Nemesis. "Talking about connections," I said one night as we were enjoying a glass of Bollinger in the sauna with Gertie, after a gruelling but enjoyable research session, "Do you remember that contortionist we saw in Nepal? That yogi who was so supple he could fellate himself. Imagine if you could hook him up to the Orgazmatron, I'm sure the direct mouth-penis contact would provide a very fruitful connection."

Gatbek didn't shout "Eureka!" but he was out of the sauna like a shot, and he returned a few minutes later with one of his spiral-bound notebooks. "Let me see," he muttered as he searched through the pages. "Katmandu, June '83, Yogi Lingabhakosa — penile diameter of four inches flaccid and five erect; flaccid length of five inches, erect length of seven inches — only seven! I beat him by at least three inches!"

I knew exactly what Gatbek was thinking of, but I must say my excitement was tinged with a peculiar premonition. However, there was no staying him from pursuing an idea once it had grabbed him by the short and curlies.

He immediately made a cushion for himself with towels on the plank floor of the sauna, lay on his back and then jerked his torso up into the yoga shoulder stand.

"Get that tape measure off my desk," he ordered. When I returned, his torso and legs were bent down over his face, with his knees and toes on the ground and the tip of his penis very close to his lips. "As I recall," he said, "of the 5,000 American white males researched by Kinsey, there were at least four who habitually masturbated by auto-fellation. And at least 60 to 70 per cent had tried! Well, to quote Bill Burroughs, wouldn't you?"

He stuck out his tongue and it just grazed the glans. "Now measure the distance from the tip to my lips."

"Inch and a half," I said.

"Good enough, I'm sure I can do it."

Next morning he contacted the most renowned yoga teacher he could find and set to work with hours of stretching and flexing exercises every day. He tied himself into pretzel shapes, practised strange breathing routines and strained and strained towards his goal. Within a month he could kiss it — just. Three weeks later my phone rang at three in the morning. "Boy, I've done it! The whole head at one swallow — and about an inch of the shaft! Come round and help me with the Orgazmatron. I can't switch it on while I'm all tied up and I need you to take notes. I also want it videotaped for the record."

"I'll be over in 15 minutes, don't try anything without me." Again I had that premonition, a nameless fear that he was going too far, that there were some things which should not be attempted. But I knew I could not dissuade him.

A thunderstorm was just breaking as I paid the cabbie and ran into the entrance hall of his apartment block. Gatbek answered the door naked — it was three a.m. and he wasn't expecting anyone else. "Come in, come in. First a drink." There were two glasses already brimming, standing ready on the table. "To the ultimate orgasm." We chinked glasses and drank. "Now, first the preliminary checks — just note my blood pressure, orgone count and pulse rate, I've already set up the Orgazmatron."

As we went through the preparations, he was as flighty as a virgin on the brink — I can't say I blamed him, I had already begun yoga training myself.

Finally all was ready: the Orgazmatron had been checked, programmed and minutely calibrated to accord with the humidity, temperature and Gatbek's ambient orgone count; the video camera was positioned on a tripod and focussed; and Gatbek's eyes were like flashing strobe lights as he attached the electrodes to nipples, the Third-eye position, his fingertips, and the nexus point we had discovered between the third and fourth vertebrae.

"I have had Escher build me a new gold-tipped dildo — better conductivity for the prostate electrode," he grinned as he greased the device and worked it up his fundament. "Now, promise me you won't terminate the experiment prematurely, even if I appear to be in agony. Often the extremes of pleasure, as you know, overlap the margins of pain. I must go the full course, even if my sanity is endangered. The pulses will build in intensity in sync with my heart rate. I've incorporated an automatic cut-out device in the circuitry in case there is any danger of cerebral overload, but given the directness of the oral-genital contact and the total involvement of all the erogenous zones, well, my boy, we are plunging into an unknown abyss."

Finally, he lay on his back on a sheepskin rug in the middle of the floor, raised his legs in a yoga shoulder stand, and then dropped them to bring his genitals close to his face. "When you see that I am fully 'engaged' count down from twenty aloud so that I may sync my breathing, then push the red switch. Ready?"

"Ready, Prof."

"Roll video."

"Video rolling, Prof."

"Energise the Orgazmatron."

"Orgazmatron energising." The LED's on the control panel fluttered, the peak meters crept up to 10,000 orgones, and a sibilant hum filled the air.

"Activate pulse generator."

"Pulse generator on." I watched the meters. "Orgazmatron and pulse-rate synced — now!"

"Geronimo!" He gripped the crook of his knees with his hands and drew his abdomen down so that the tip of his penis entered his mouth — he was extraordinarily supple.

"Twenty, nineteen, eighteen, seventeen . . ."

Although his chest was compressed I could see he was breathing rhythmically. "Sixteen, fifteen, fourteen, thirteen . . . " He winked at me then closed his eyes.

"Twelve, eleven, ten . . . " Outside I heard a crack of thunder, then the rain beat upon the windows and the wind howled. "Nine, eight, seven, six, five, four . . . "

I could feel my own heart pounding in my chest — I was about to witness history.

"Three, two, one . . . " A deep breath, then: "Zero!"

I pushed the red switch.

Immediately the hum of the orgazmatron rose to a shriek, all his muscles flexed and twitched, sweat beads prickled out all over his naked flesh, and his whole body went into spasms. The lights on the control panel were flashing faster and faster, and his body flexed and shuddered in sync. His eyeballs bulged white and staring, his curly hair seemed to be standing on end, the cords were standing out on his straining neck, his lips were drawn into a lurid grimace, fluid began to gush from his mouth, and his torso flexed and tensed in a series of convulsions that drove his member ever deeper . . .

There was an almighty flash that blinded me, and I was flung across the room as the crash reverberated through the apartment.

I must have blacked out. When I regained consciousness I was dazed. There was a smell like an electrical ozone discharge mixed with burning — 'Pork?' I thought to myself confusedly, before I realised the odour was charred human flesh — I was familiar with the smell from our adventures in the Amazon Basin.

"Gatbek, Gatbek!" As I rose dizzily, glass from the shattered penthouse windows crunched under my feet — a torrent of rain lashed in and the rolling and crashing thunder seemed like angry laughter. All the lights had gone out but by the flashes of lightning outside I could make out the professor's twisted form, and the expression on his face will live with me until the day I die.

I thought quickly, grabbed what I had to and fled. Outside all was confusion. The whole of Sydney was in darkness — it was like the wartime blackout all over again — only the lights of police vehicles, ambulances and taxis scything through the storm-lashed streets. People were running and yelling wildly in utter panic. I heard screams and the screech and crash of vehicles coming to grief. Gatbek's ultimate orgasm had unleashed — or coincided with — what felt like a minor apocalypse of pent-up emotions, psychic fury and hysteria. How I got back to my own apartment I'll never know. I drank a double whisky and took a triple dose of sleeping pills to blot out consciousness before collapsing on my bed.

That was three months ago. I have analysed Gatbek's notebooks and persuaded Escher, the electronics expert who helped him build the Orgazmatron, to help me duplicate and improve on the device. It is ready — and so am I. I was never as supple or as well-endowed as the professor, but those long hours in the gym and the ashram have paid off. It is within my grasp — just a kiss away. When I have finished this account of Gatbek's spectacular end, I shall set the video cameras rolling, adjust the Orgazmatron II to automatic, attach and insert the electrodes, and begin the countdown . . .

You see, although Gatbek's face was charred, and blue flames actually flickered in the sockets where his eyes had been, he died smiling, smiling smiling — like the Cheshire cat that ate . . . itself.

EDWARD McCANN

A Pleasure Dome Decreed

It is not considered good form these days to murder your builder. A lot of it went on during the Nile Kingdoms, or so we are led to believe. Unruly bricklayers and their builders being immured in Pharaoh's tomb. Trapped for all eternity into doing his bidding. Building vaster and vaster pyramids across the endless sands of the hereafter. That was Pharaoh's prerogative and he had more money than Jeremy. That was Luxor, this Drummoyne. Here the builder is protected by such august bodies as the Building Workers Union, the Builders' Registration Board, numerous federal, state and local government ordinances and one of the ten commandments. Yet Jeremy, throwing his bonnet over the mill and all caution to the winds, murdered his. Crushed his skull with a corded sash weight and thus did kill him.

> *"Ittim on the head*
> *Wiffa fuckin' lump of lead*
> *Now they say 'es dead*
> *I killdim."*

Jeremy sat in his newly renovated, completely finished, at long last, living room, with en suite kitchen and wriggled his toes as he sang softly to himself the old convict song. He rocked in front of his fire and the flames from the blazing logs flickered and reflected against the richly varnished panellings. The wind howled around the chimney, sending down patters of rain to hiss and spit against the burnished copper canopy. His stained glass french doors twinkled out to a palm fringed patio of raised and sunken fern gardens, where the rain deluged down as it had for thirty six days and nights of heavy showers with intermittent thunderstorms. He sipped on his goblet of port and looked about him. The discreet lighting made his painted walls and pictures glow. His highly waxed floors reflected the glow on his flushed and satisfied cheeks.

Jeremy re-arranged some plans on his knees and click, clack computed on his wrist watch. No mistake. It was only thirteen months and twenty six days since the builder had agreed to complete Jeremy's renovations, to Jeremy's specifications, in four weeks. . . It seemed like a lifetime. He endured all those months, days, weeks and hours of frustrated misery with a calm and fortitude he and his friends could only wonder at.

> *"Oh they say I'll do my time*
> *Do my time, do my time*
> *Finish on the line, then a pit of burning lime*
> *I killdim."*

Like marriage, home renovations should not be entered into lightly. The mating preliminaries are basically the same. The two future partners are wary at first. They circle each other for a while. They have both been wounded in the past. Then, like lyrebirds mating, there is a flamboyant show of their respective good points. In the builder's case it takes the form of trade papers or a resume of past projects. With the householder, it is basically legible plans and money, to advance.

Over a few beers at the kitchen table, Jeremy and the builder discussed the whole project again before making their final commitment. Jeremy spread his arms like someone playing a large accordion. The confining walls and pokey little windows, with cracked louvres, fell away and were replaced with elegantly sliding glass panels leading out to his landscaped garden. He pointed to the plans he had drawn up himself. Every detail and parameter depicted in exquisite proportion. Jeremy made many references to his wrist computer, as they projected and agreed on the amount and cost of raw materials and labour. A commitment was required and freely given, as to the definition of a week, a day, an hour. Firm purpose was applied as to how long the project would take to complete. Subject to the availability of materials, clemency of weather and other unforeseen obstacles, agreement was reached. Documents were drawn up and mutually signed. Binding them together with the rigidity of a Greek marriage contract.

Jeremy broke out a bottle of the good rum and they drank it under the clothes hoist in the little back yard which would soon become a pleasure dome filled with brightly coloured birds and moths — flitting, weaving and bobbing like diamond flashes through the waving fronds of the exotic plants and blooms. While fragrant essence from a clutch of incense wandered across the form of Lord Buddha and chimes played to the kiss of the wind. Peace, contentment, bliss.

As the builder toiled in Jeremy's backyard, Jeremy laboured in the city. However he found difficulty concentrating his thoughts, as his mind constantly drifted towards the builder. Where was he now? Was he climbing the roof and removing the old tin preparatory to demolishing the bathroom? Or was he stacking the timber in his slow methodical way, so as it would ready at his hand for using? A true craftsman, thought Jeremy, will not be rushed.

There was lots to be done before the actual building. Jeremy had not removed as many plants as the builder had requested. Consequently the builder removed them himself. This caused some damage which Jeremy noticed. As there was not much doing at work which could not be delegated, Jeremy took to starting late of a morning and finishing early in the afternoon. Just to give the builder a hand in getting started. It was fun to strip down to shorts, don big boots and sweat the sedentary flab from a body too long behind a desk. By clearing up the mounds of sawdust, offcuts and rubble it took the edge off and allowed the builder to devote his time building. This appeared to be so successful Jeremy, took his holidays early in order to devote more time to the project.

By the third hour, of the first day, of the second working week, the builder had not arrived. Jeremy, reluctantly but dutifully, after computing it on his wrist, noted it in his ledger. The sun was screened behind low lying cloud. The temperature was pleasant, with a little breeze. Enough to cool the brow, yet not too gusty to blow the grit and dust about. It was a perfect day which Jeremy used to tidy up the yard, re-stack the timber and do some weeding. He prepared some sandwiches in anticipation of a shared lunch. Then as the afternoon closed to a chill evening he made a large jug of Bonox to which he added a few goodly tots of rum. Pulling on a warm jumper, he sat, sipped and brooded.

On the morning of the third day the builder returned. Whistling, then smiling broadly, as if he were just turning the corner and had never been away. There was a story about some old customer with a heart condition who just had to have his roof replaced before he came out of hospital. How there was the complication of termites. He had meant to ring. Had asked Sonia, his lady, but she was so busy, what with the baby and her classes, never got round to it. A couple more days would see the old mate sweet. Then he would get back to Jeremy and they would hoe into it. Meanwhile he ripped the weather wall off the kitchen, leaving Jeremy to clean up. Friday was the long weekend and nobody worked then. The builder arrived back by the middle of the next week, when Jeremy, his holidays over, was reluctantly back at work. Again using the chainsaw, he this time removed the back of the house. Leaving the mess, thought Jeremy, as a kind of calling card. Four days later he knocked down most of the bathroom and toilet. This was how things remained for the next few months.

Jeremy phoned frequently, sometimes getting past Sonia to the builder. "First thing in the morning," then "As soon as the bricks arrive," and "We're held up till we get the runners from Germany. You will get those funny windows. Should have made them from cedar as I suggested."

Late winter turned to spring, wet summer and autumn and before Jeremy knew, early winter. Still the elements whistled, gusted and wrought havoc through his apartments. They rattled the paintings on the walls and blew dead dreams across the floors with the dried leaves and swirling dust for Jeremy to clean up of a lonely evening.

Jeremy spent his free weekends tacking on weatherboard and laying bricks. Only to have his work ripped out and torn down when the builder deigned to appear, as it did not come up to his exacting standards. Occasionally they would have their good days. Ripping into it and perhaps tarring a roof. Then standing in the late afternoon under a sun warmed shower and rubbing each other's black streaked bodies with Solvol soap. Until Sonia would call. Something about the baby choking or not eating. What should she do? And would he pick up some Kimbies from the supermarket on the way home, or was he going to drink there all night?

He was feeling neglected. The builder had not turned up again. The project appeared to be little changed from when they first started. The kitchen was in tatters with the wind continually blowing out the gas. His bathroom and toilet were exposed on all sides, the water pipes writhing in the air like the ganglia of Jeremy's tormented nerves. Large sheets of torn plastic flapped sadly across the missing main wall of his living room. Furniture which did not fit was scattered through the other rooms. The resulting ensemble jarred the eye and made movement difficult. He never invited anyone over for dinner anymore and those little luncheons on a Sunday were a dim, pleasant memory. The only person to share his table, break his bread and drink his wine, was the builder, when he came to visit. Jeremy had suffered enough. He felt humiliated, abused and compromised. He and the builder had sat at this very table and agreed. Made their covenant. Drank to it. How many months ago? Jeremy clicked his wrist. Then reached for the phone.

The builder was drunk and stoned. In the background of their conversation could be heard the cacophony of blaring television and bawling child. Jeremy imagined the floor of the builder's hovel to be covered in discarded Kimbies and could almost smell the fish fingers and brussel sprouts which Sonia was surely overcooking.

Jeremy could be quite brutal. He had not reached his rung on the corporate ladder with unbloodied hands. The builder was sacked. He made excuses. The weather. Jeremy's changes. Jeremy was adamant. The builder pleaded. He was a craftsman. He had put and intended to put much more of himself into the project. After a lot of fumblings and false starts, tomorrow would be his renaissance. Jeremy was firm. The builder wept. Sonia, the baby. Jeremy did not know what it was like. He had three other jobs going as well as Jeremy's. He had to keep everyone happy and make ends meet. Jeremy wilted. Finally they agreed. "In the morning."

For the next two days the weather was perfect. It was raining when the builder eventually turned up late afternoon on the third day. Jeremy was waiting. He could not go to work until it was resolved and called in sick, as he was. The builder was drunk. Before Jeremy could smell the stench of beer and White Ox tobacco, that much was obvious. The builder stumbled across the neatly stacked timber and heaped rubble which Jeremy had placed against the fence. The timber fell with a clatter and rubble spewed across the path. Jeremy's mouth was like a stretched string as he watched from the top of where his back steps used to be. What should have been a fern garden was a demolition site of long standing. He could not use his shower or toilet as the neighbours complained to the council about the forced intimacy of his ablutions. Clutching a long list of what he perceived to be the builder's sins of omission and commission, Jeremy jumped down into the yard. He stumbled and fell. A bad start. He was almost as drunk as the builder.

The builder was arrogant drunk. What right had Jeremy to sack him, after all he had put into the project? It had taken time, sure . This was a job which would last. In years to come Jeremy could rest his weariness beneath the shade of palms and tree ferns. Jeremy demurred that perhaps his grandchildren would. The builder expressed his doubts as to Jeremy's inclination or ability to sire any. Rather than be embroiled in such puerile bickerings, Jeremy stuck to his list, enumerating its demerits. The builder was aghast, dismissing Jeremy's allegations out of hand. Jeremy relentlessly ticked off all the items while the builder interjected. He ended with his misgivings concerning the efficacy of the drainage system. The way in which the downfall from the roof gutter emptied into the ditch around the retaining wall of his raised garden was such that the rain would eventually weaken and cause its collapse. The builder was outraged. What would Jeremy know of such things? All he was fit for was to sit on his fat arse and fiddle with his wrist computer. He should stay in his office, filled with girls who were scared of him and leave the work to real men. He gave Jeremy a push, causing him to fall amongst the scattered rubble. All the months of anger and pent up frustration were suddenly released. All his school years of taunted misery, because of his pudgy frame, exploded with the force of a bursting boil. He scrabbled on his back, an upturned crab, till his fingers came in contact with a long hardness. He grabbed the corded sash weight and lost his thongs. Nails and broken glass among the rubble slashed his feet as he stumbled upright. Swinging the sash weight around his head, he smashed the builder's cheek to the bone. He fell to the ground and Jeremy continued the battering long after he had finished gurgling and was still.

The sun dribbled behind the neighbour's fence and eventually Jeremy roused himself. The builder's broken body was sprawled across some four-by-twos. Maybe he could say he fell? Looking at the long deep contusions on the builder's face and head, he dismissed the idea. He glanced furtively around the yard. They were screened from the neighbour's view. As there were no anxious inquiries from beyond, the fight had apparently gone unnoticed. Those who were not at work, were shopping or preparing the evening meal.

Removing the builder's boots and heavy socks, Jeremy laid them reverently by his side. When the striped jersey and shorts joined them, the builder looked so pathetic and helpless. What shortly before had been so formidably intimidating was now reduced to a bundle of soiled clothes and scattered limbs. He lay across the pile of rubble with his head thrown back and his mouth slightly open. As relaxed and beautiful as a herd boy Jeremy had stumbled across once on a thyme-scented hillside on Corfu.

Jeremy battered out those teeth still left in the builder's

mouth. Weeping, he rearranged the features and with a Stanley knife hacked off the scalp. Then he removed the genitalia and the hair from the pubis, chest and armpits. Finally he coated the hands, fingers and limbs with the acid used to degrease the galvanised iron. All he removed was placed in a heap with the clothes, to be burned when those around slept.

Jeremy cleared the rubble from the area of his largest raised garden. He dug a deep hole and after looking around folded the builder in. Lying on his side, with his knees drawn up, he reminded Jeremy of a Bronze Age warrior in his barrow. After filling the hole in gently with rich loam, Jeremy planted a large tree fern on top. He then placed some large stones around it, stripped off his bloody clothes and took a long soapy shower. "Bugger the neighbours." he said defiantly at the blue flickering windows.

> *"Now when the parson comes, parson comes*
> *E'll speak of the life ahead*
> *I'll say take my fuckin' place instead*
> *I killdim."*

Jeremy finished his little song and sniffed the air. It was redolent with the smell of fresh varnish mixed with a vindaloo chicken he had simmering in his crock pot. The rain would ease off during the night. According to the weatherman it would be fine for his luncheon guests on the morrow. He had invited Nora, his secretary, Mr Lumsden, his boss, Mona, his wife, Mother, and the new junior executive from advertising, who with a helping hand and a prod in the right direction could go far.

Thank God all that building was finished. After he had disposed of the builder his life had been made a misery by Sonia's incessant ringing. Her voice had whined for days over the phone. Where was he? When had Jeremy seen him last? He told her exactly as he told the police when they called. The builder was supposed to come on the Monday, he hadn't and Jeremy had not spoken to him since he had sacked him. Sonia confirmed the call and the sacking. The police, after looking at the mess and digging into the builder's affairs decided that it had all become too much for him. He was probably up in Andamooka or somewhere digging opals.

Jeremy employed a young carpenter from the Commonwealth Employment Service who finished the job off to his satisfaction. He came promptly of a morning and did more in a day than the builder had in a week. He kept him well away from the tree fern, which was flourishing, and before he had gotten to know the lad, or found out if he had a middle name or girlfriend, the project was completed exactly as Jeremy had visualised and he was gone.

Switching the crock pot down to a low simmer, Jeremy went to bed with Sitwell's *English Eccentrics.*

By noon the basmati rice was in the steamer and the vindaloo filled the house with its fragrance. The clouds had rolled away and the sparkling leaves soon dry. Jeremy arranged seating around the tree fern, lit mosquito coils and incense, then busied himself making sangria. By 1pm all the quests had dribbled in and he gave the task of changing tapes to the junior executive. Unfortunately his taste tended towards heavy metal, which Jeremy kept for other occasions. After the guests were primed with the sangria and his mother seated on the armed chair at the head of the table, Jeremy quietly changed the tape to the delightful Oul Kousoum's sensual caterwauling of life and love. She blended well with the palms, ferns and incense which drifted in fine ectoplasmic wisps through their foliage.

Jeremy's boss bent to sniff a bloom and asked its name. *"Hedychium Garneriadum,"* replied Jeremy. "I'll give you a bulb when it's stopped blooming." His boss smiled his appreciation at Jeremy's knowledge. "Snip off a bloom and give it to Mum," he suggested. His boss plucked one of the deep yellow blossoms and presented it with a flourish and elegant bow to the old lady. Jeremy's mum took it, giving in return a courtly nod of her head. She and everyone else jumped at a thudding noise as if someone had dumped a bag of coal on the path. There was a rushing sound as a large volume of earth cascaded over the collapsed retaining wall. The tree fern swayed to the side like a drunken sailor. And the builder's rotten fleshed arm fell negligently across the secretary's shoulder, like that of an old friend.

"I told him this would happen," said Jeremy calmly as he continued to spoon out the vindaloo.

15+

He was a child of another climate. His early years were urban, working class and relentlessly coastal.

He lived only minutes from the sea but wished his suburb rid of its influence. The sea that brought its taste to his table and its tourists to his street, their fibreglass fins bundling their burning into steaming back seats.

The sea that formed on every surface, the paint that hung from houses and shops, the rust of fenders, the white flakes that would appear under his fringe and fingernails. All around him, the world was shedding its skin while he would have given the world to shed his.

He would burn. Easily. Often. The clouds would separate for a second and he would burn. A shirt collar strayed from a shoulder and he would burn. A blow dryer switched on in a neighbouring suburb and he would burn.

His suffering was never recognised until his complexion was numbered, labelled and categorised.

15+

He liked the sound of it. 'Fair' had always suggested lack while this implied abundance.

He was less enthusiastic when he discovered that, in his case, 15+ referred not only to the strength of the lotion but also to the number of necessary applications.

Once inside his bedroom, the oceans would cease. He covered the windows and walls with rainforests dripping with leaves, mountains collapsing into valleys, snatches of mist that rose from ravines and floated above his wardrobe.

He did, however, make one concession to the coast. On the back of his bedroom door, a row of lifesavers flattered the beach only a block away. His mother enquired as to his interest in the newspaper report. He explained that these men shared a complexion and a physique to which he aspired, a story he found difficult to support when the paper was found folded beside his bed, the pages clinging together.

It occurred to him that the answer might be no further than the kitchen cupboard. He swung open the doors and scanned the collection of bottles and canisters containing powders and liquids in various shades of brown. He bundled them into his schoolcase and hid them in his bedroom.

Over the following day, his approach was entirely scientific. He prepared the mixtures with tap water, each time altering the amount of liquid before he applied it to his skin. He deleted peanut butter early in the survey as it lacked the desired consistency and colour. Coffee and Milo failed to leave an authentic and durable stain. His experiments with barbeque sauce and Gravox were particularly successful although they did tend to leave a conspicuous odour.

His mother began to notice the gaps in the pantry and reprimanded him for his gluttony. Shortly after, she found him in the bathroom smearing soggy Coco Pops into his chest. It was then that she realised that he was not so much eating the groceries as wearing them.

On the 26th of January, 1970, Captain Cook, a chubby boy with premature acne, was being rowed ashore by the local lifesavers. A handful of children sat behind him, dressed as characters of the currency.

He stood on the foreshore, an aboriginal with boot polish, teased hair and a tea-towel loincloth. He had been rehearsing the part for weeks after missing out on Henry Lawson by a narrow margin. He had never met an aboriginal before but he was coached in a dialect he was assured would sound authentic. Whenever he felt compelled to speak, he only had to say, "Wagga wagga kumbi umbi woy woy wollongong."

When the party had assembled on the sand, he took his cue and walked forward with the half dozen that made up his tribe, extending his hand in greeting. So overwhelming was the welcome that he was pushed up against Captain Cook who steadied himself, looked down at the black smudge on his military dress and burst into tears. A moment later, he found himself dazed, looking up, his black face freckled with sand.

Bennelong had Henry Lawson in a headlock. The portrait Namatjira was to present to the colonials sat torn across Joseph Bank's shoulders. Governor Macarthur was being carried away screaming by his parents while his own mother and father did not intervene until it seemed as if Caroline

Chisolm was trying to drown him in the shallow surf.

It came with the promise of a new skin. He needed only unscrew the cap and it would be his. Indoor. Overnight. Roll on complexion. Roll on arms. Roll on legs. Roll on torso. Roll on sheets, blankets, pyjamas and pillow cases. Roll on everything but him.

His morning skin seemed the same as the evening before, although the palms of his hands had turned an interesting orange.

Christmas lunch under a beach umbrella. Relatives, red-faced, beer bellied, slapping shoulders, swapping stories and passing plates of chicken and coleslaw.

He could not eat. He was used to a Yuletide swelter but this day the barometer was bursting. When no-one was looking, he opened the esky and held his face above a shaft of cool air.

He stared across the empty esplanade, down the mall quivering in the silver heat, past shops, houses, streets, mountains, seas and continents to a living room in the North Pole. Santa Claus sat by the fire, weary from a night's work. He wished this time the old man had taken him along, snatched him from his sleep to ride across rooftops to a home in a place where the ocean would freeze and the sun stayed for months.

He turned back to the beach and watched Santa emerge from the dressing shed, wearing a red and white cap with matching Speedos. A crowd of cousins ran and wrestled for places around Saint Nick who reached into a hessian sack. He, however, held back respectfully at the edge of the crowd and examined the man for a moment. There was something in that face sweating beneath the white beard that seemed to resemble his own. He wanted to run back to his father and ask if Santa might be kin but as he looked back to the cluster of umbrellas, Dad was nowhere to be seen.

He turned back to see a large red box inches from his face. He thanked Santa who replied with a wink of familiarity. Tearing through the layers of paper, cardboard and tissue, he stared shocked at what the wrappings revealed — a bucket and spade, a snorkel and mask and a crumpled kaleidoscope of inflatable rubber, all this from the man he had hoped would deliver him from the tyranny of the coast. He threw the box and himself on the ground, pounding his fists into the sand.

Beneath an umbrella, a transistor radio crooned, 'May all your Christmases be white.'

He had dreamed of a place where a complexion such as his might be celebrated, or of a time when his freckles would form an even brown. One night his sleep suggested that the land masses might expand, the continents congeal, and heal the vast wound that separated them. Slowly, he began to realise that his enemy was not his skin, not even the sun, but the communities that would cling to the coast line and their dreams of owning a piece of it.

One night he dreamt that God had erased the beaches from his grand design. The next day, he woke to a suburb standing on its side. Telephone poles lay across the gutters like discarded needle and thread and cars offered up their underbellies. During the night, a gale had moved between the houses, gathering fences, gardens, letter boxes, unsettling everything but his sleep.

As usual, he walked to school down Ocean View Drive. Approaching the edge of the esplanade, he gathered pace and threw himself against the railing, staring, screaming. He saw a beach stripped to its bones, shedding sand with every wave. He looked up into the cloudy heavens, in awe of the power of his dreams.

GRAEME AITKEN

Aiming for an Encore

I discovered when I finally woke up, late afternoon, that I was actually in my own bed, wearing nothing apart from somebody else's leather jacket and a condom on my dick. I took off the jacket to admire it, and a card fell out of the pocket. I picked it up. "Call me — 51 2760." I screwed it up, and pulled off the condom. It was broken.

I met him at one of the summer dance parties. I remember lying outside on the damp grass, watching the laser lights track across the sky, and then Joey slips something into my mouth, and after a while the lights get to be kind of fascinating, and I am floating.

The number had been written on the back of a ticket from the dance party. Strange. I never go to them these days. Three years ago, for sure. All the time, and all night long. Now that was when they were hot. Before they got to be so mainstream. Before they became the only thing people seem to talk about in this city. Still, I guess I must've gone along.

I was lying on the grass and floating up to meet the moon at the same time, and needing something to drink like crazy. So I sit up and look around, but can't remember where the bar is. But then I can't remember where I've put my money either. I don't seem to have any pockets. In fact, I don't seem to have much on.

Then I see Tab. He grins at me, and so I run over and fling my arms around his neck and start to kiss him. And Tab is running his hands all over me, and I'm hoping he'll come across my money, 'cause I'm desperate for something to drink. But then Tab would buy me a drink. We are old friends. Old fucks.

I open my eyes and look up into his . . . and suddenly realise . . . that something isn't quite right. I am looking up for a start . . . but I am taller than Tab, and I'm looking into blue eyes, and Tab's eyes are . . . they're . . . well, they're certainly not blue. I step back and have a good look, and he stares right on back. This is not Tab but it doesn't particularly matter. I press up against him, feeling kind of coy and ask, "Would you buy me a mineral water or something?"

"Sure," he says, and starts kissing me again, and after a while I just forget that I'm feeling so thirsty.

I was beginning to wish I'd been too hung over to notice the bloody ticket. I was wishing my eyes had been incapable of focusing and recognising the stupid phone number. I had screwed it up and tossed it away immediately, and tried to go back to sleep and convince myself it was a dream.

As if I could. I had memorised it. I couldn't help myself. I just do things like that, though I wish I wouldn't. Now that number was going to nag at me unrelentingly. Because, there had to be a name attached to that number, and a face . . . and a body . . . and I had to know.

Though of course, I wouldn't dial the number. I couldn't. Instead that phone number would cling stubbornly inside my head for weeks, probably months, until I met someone capable of distracting me long enough to forget about it.

I knew this routine only too well.

I can't remember how we got to his place, and I didn't know where we were. I did ask him, but he just laughs, and says, "In bed."

And we were. But that wasn't what I meant. And I tried to explain, but he was kissing me again and tugging at my shorts. I suddenly had this really urgent idea that I wanted to dance, and I couldn't understand why I'd left the party in the first place, when I was having such a good time and all my friends were there. But maybe this wouldn't last very long, and I could go back again. And maybe I wouldn't be able to get an erection, but then he yanked my shorts right down past my knees, and much to my surprise, I had one already. And so did he. Then he was on top of me and unscrewing the amyl bottle with his teeth, and I was beginning to

I couldn't get back to sleep. I had this dull ache (and his
bloody phone number) echoing through my brain, and I needed to take a piss. I lay there for about an hour willing it all to go
away, but it didn't. So I got out of bed and headed for the
bathroom. Checked my records on the way. I lost all my Abba
albums to some North Shore blonde I met at Patches last year.

Found some pills in the bathroom that looked like Pana-
dol (they had a 'P' on them), so I took those, had a piss and
then sat down on the toilet to think about things. Should I take
a shower? Was I hungry? Maybe ring up Greg and see if he knew
what I did last night? Or who I was with?
I pulled off the jacket, and turned on the shower, and . . .
the jacket. I looked at it lying crumpled on the lino. There was
cum all up the front of it. My cum? Maybe. I must've withdrawn
then before I came . . . before the condom broke . . . and maybe
we didn't even fuck . . . and did I do it ? Or did he ? But I was the
one wearing the fucking faulty thing, so it must've been me.
And I knew that condom would torment me into having a test
and I'd go through agonies for three months. But there was
cum on the jacket, instead of in him. And it had to be mine. My
cum on his jacket. His jacket.
If I needed an excuse to call, then I had one. Not that I
needed one. I would give him a call for the hell of it.

It was his of course, the jacket. Shame. I was hoping that
maybe the cloak check had made a fabulous mistake. Of
course, he wanted me to come straight on over, but I just
laughed, and he said, "Dinner then. Let's have a late dinner
tonight."

Obviously, I'd 'performed', if he wanted an encore this
quickly. But I told him I was tired and suggested a drink.
"Tomorrow night," he insisted, and I said "Okay."

Frankly, I didn't want to touch another drink (or another
cock) for a couple of weeks, months even . . . though the
swelling in my jocks would seem to contradict me.

Eventually, he comes out of the dressing room, very subdued, and I know I won't have any trouble getting him to front up with the cash. I threaten to call the manager and he brings out his wallet. I overcharge him $30.00 for the jeans (which were a shocking fit), but I reckon I deserve it.

I make one more sale all day. Some business type who insists I choose an entire outfit for him. I select the most expensive items in the shop. He pays for it all with a gold Amex card and admires my taste. I agree, though I'd never be seen wearing any of the stuff we stock.

I close up the shop after making that big sale, and go home for a nap before the date. I haven't had a date in a while, and it makes me feel like jerking off, but I save it and go to sleep instead. Just in case.

I went to a free performance for the unemployed at Belvoir Street Theatre this afternoon. It was a play I'd auditioned for several months previously, and somehow had been overlooked for the part. It was infuriating. The guy who did get it was so . . . adequate. I knew if I'd been given the chance I would've been compelling.

And then I would've been able to invite him along to see me, instead of going for a drink. I could've mentioned it very casually. "Oh by the way, I'm in a play." And he would've come along and insisted on a front row seat, where he'd sit forward throughout, his eyes always following me, in awe, almost frightened by the fierce energy of my performance. Afterwards, he would wait impatiently for me, striding across the foyer, tossing down drinks, and then finally when I emerged, he would seize my hands, and spill out his praises, his eyes glowing with admiration.

He brought the leather jacket along with him, which surprised me. I was sure he'd leave it at home, as an excuse to lure me back there. Just as well he did bring it though, 'cause I wouldn't have known which expectant guy to sit down with otherwise.

He orders me a drink, and I don't know what else to say after thanks. Suddenly, I feel very sober indeed. I drink it down fast.

All I could think about when he first sat down was that I had never seen him before, though I must've had his cock in my mouth less than thirty six hours ago.

After the second drink, we begin to talk more, or rather he begins to talk about some play he's in or something and I listen. It sounds as boring as he is. But, of course, being an actor, he is cute.

I was having to do all the work. He at least was buying the drinks.

I arrived late so we'd only have to talk for half an hour before the bar closed. Come midnight, I know he wants to ask me home, but he suggests we swap phone numbers instead and says he'll call me. He didn't pay for a single drink either.

He said he'd give me a call soon and I said sure.

I wear the leather jacket to work all week. I can't believe my luck. The manager points out Friday that there is a bit of a stain down the front.

I was beginning to feel quite excited about seeing him again. The fact that I couldn't remember sleeping with him, made it all so much more romantic. It was like we were dating and waiting for the sex, so that it would be something special. I knew that we'd ring each other up and laugh and chat about nothing in particular, just for the sake of it. We'd go out for leisurely dinners at tables for two, our eyes duelling across plates of spicy food, our conversation flushed with desire. And afterwards, we'd kiss hopelessly on street corners, thrilled by the fact that we would go home alone.

Until, finally, one night, we would linger in our farewell and he would shyly confide the utter trust that he has in me. And I would wrap him up in my embraces and sweep him home without any hesitations, without a word being spoken, but with the utter conviction of a lover.

*Of course, I don't ring him. I mean, I just can't. I go to see
the play he mentioned instead. I figure we can meet up afterwards, casually.*

*But he's not in it. His name isn't even in the programme.
Either I wasn't listening to him properly (and I wasn't) or else he
was having me on. Whatever, I'm $20.00 down after buying the
ticket to go, and totally unimpressed. I'm certainly not about to
ring him now.*

I wasn't exactly waiting for him to ring, but I was aware
that he didn't. Still, I found the erotic uncertainty of our situation rather exciting. I knew he'd be getting off on this game as
well, savouring this silence, delighting in drawing out this
tension between us for another hour, another day. I knew he
would be sitting at home, beside the phone, thinking of me,
with an erection as big as the receiver.

*I have this feeling he'll show up at Dome for Tuesday night.
He said he liked it there. So I go along, and he doesn't show. I
meet up with an information technologist from Eastwood instead.*

It would be refreshing for once to meet someone who
proved to be telephone literate. I mean someone capable of
picking up the phone and dialling a seven digit number. Why is
it that so many boys are only capable of passively picking up
the telephone when the fucking thing rings? (Which it never
does here incidently). I don't even care if he can't make
conversation. The fact that he actually thought of me, and
dialled my number would be enough.

Not that I'm so petty as to insist that it was his turn to
ring, because I rang him last time. But the point was that I had.

*After two weeks had gone by, I rip up his number and forget
that it's in the book anyway. I keep on wearing the leather jacket,
which I have had deep cleaned.*

IAN MacNEILL

As the Cold War Rages
Along Oxford Street

I sit in the bar of the Albury watching. Outside it is cold and blustery, inside . . .

Snake-eyes in the 501's is eyeing me off. I like him, he looks as though he has a big cock. Anyway, he's a big man. Got to have something.

His eyes bore into me. If I smile I know I'll spoil everything for him.

He heads towards the toilets, giving me a look.

I'm almost tempted — to see what he's got. Then I think about the escape and how bad I'll feel whenever I'll see him again. And I will see him again. And I will, I will.

Gerard would have said, 'That tells me everything about him.' But where is Gerard right now?

It's just me and the Albury. All these guys. All these guys talking, looking, laughing. I've been one of them, looking at some guy and thinking he's a closet from the suburbs in for a desperate Sunday afternoon. 'Church didn't work this morning, eh bud? Still got the Saturday night hots?' Joke Joyce.

Snake-eyes comes out of the toilet and it's as if nothing has happened. Poor guy. Perhaps it's just my paranoia, my fantasy, or something, Who am I kidding?

A guy near me is perched on one of those stools designed for Gary Cooper (Gerard), reading *OutRage*. It's got a guy on the cover. He looks a bit like me. Like everyone. They're looking for Mr. Gay Australia. I hope they find him. The one on the cover looks O.K. Gerard would say, 'Put your shirt on honey.'

A couple of eunuchs are talking about sex near me. (I must remember that for Gerard). One of them is a teacher in a private school — Newington? He's talking about some kid in the rowing-team. Jesus. You ought to see him — the twank — I mean, he's a bad forty. The kid he's frothing over is blond (you guessed it), tall (ditto), really nice (that's fresh) and — do my ears deceive me? — fifteen. Jesus. I was fifteen once. So was he. Jesus. I wonder what he did to deserve to end up like that? I wonder what I'll end up like? I won't be sitting here in any case.

Not that anywhere else is better. Some people think some places are better but that's just because they know the crowd there.

The newsflasher is telling us all about the big week ahead in the Albury. God it sounds terrific. There's going to be some drag queens doing an AIDS benefit for Bobby Goldsmith. Some of us here could do with a benefit.

I'm drinking beer with a peppermint schnapps chaser. So my breath won't go sour and bitter on me — or anyone else.

I think I'll go into the other bar. It's amazing. I always wish I was stoned in here. There are these palm trees made out of brass, only life-sized — well almost.

A few happy tragics are sipping cocktails with little umbrellas and plastic mermaids clinging to the edge of these big glasses. I hope they ask me to join them for a drink. Where are their manners? Don't they watch old movies?

They don't. Having too good a time.

Perhaps I don't look . . .

No-one is playing the big black piano with the mike hanging where the pianist's face should be. I feel I'd like to sit down and play but I don't know how and I can't think of the words to any songs — except nursery rhymes — little boy blue come blow on your horn.

I go back in to see . . .

Nothing's happening. The flasher's telling us about the drag show at nine and eleven on Tuesday. I'm the only one who ever reads it and I hardly ever get to see the shows. Come at the wrong times I guess.

I just order another peppermint schnapps. The barman's a real queen. I like him a whole lot better than the macho queens who think they're doing you a favour if they serve you. But this one's tripping on it too. He thinks he's a tv show host. God he's shrieking. Must be new to the job.

I might try the Unicorn. It's cold out there. It looks like rain.

Snake-eyes looks happy. The grog must be getting to his balls, now they're warm he can let them swing. He's talking to someone — must be a mate of his — the sort of person he'd never get off with. Actually he gets off for .00027 of a millisec in toilets. I wonder when the moment is? I wish I'd gone with him,

I might have been able to spot it, maybe he rolls his eyes or something. I bet the only time he actually comes is when he's at home and wanking over Playboy or something. Probably Mummy told him never to play with girls and beat the shit out of him when she caught him with his sister under the house. I can't stand these non-gay types.

I think I'll drag my peppermint schnapps back to the cocktail party.

They've gone. Must have dropped in for a quick drink. Must be on their way to the opera or something. I'd like to go to the movies. I wonder what's on? If it's too late. I could ask someone to go with me. Who?

I wish they had a drag show.

I might go next door into Cappucino City to have a coffee. Maybe I could talk to someone in there. I could sit in the window and watch to see if any of my friends or anyone I know walks by. Maybe the waiter'd be friendly. Maybe the cocktail party's adjourned for cake and coffee and there'll be no spare tables and I could . . .

That's the schnapps. God it clears your sinuses, the nasal passages.

I guess it's time to go. I can breathe all that strong, clear, cold air on my way back.

Perhaps I'll go upstairs and see if Gerard's back yet. He might feel like a cup of coffee.

Corrugated Lives

PRE-POST ADOLESCENCE

Jordy lived in a Pre-post era. Pre-post Modernism, Pre-post Colonialism and Pre-post 'person'. In his neighbourhood, he had a 'postie' and a pet dachshund who once had a bad experience with a bicycle. The Townsends always knew when their endowment cheque had arrived. The postie didn't blow the whistle.

A FRAGILE CHILD

"I DON'T WANT TO GO TO THE FUCKING CIRCUS ANY-WAY," were Jordy's final words on the matter. As his father rose from his seat, he put down his newspaper, meticulous in his care of fold. Jordy, smug and arms crossed, stuck out his chin in a gesture to embrace punishment. His parents passed each other in the hall, less than strangers. The key of the study barely clicked. The door locked and Mr Townsend was out of sight. A well-oiled interchange. Mrs Townsend entered with a tray of brandy snaps. Her eyes were 25 watt incandescent with glee. Jordy stuck his finger down his throat, dry-retching and belching until she fled the room. Parents properly berated, Jordy then proceeded to eat the brandy snaps. Jordy watched *Evil Dead* for the twenty seventh time. 'Dead Boring,' he thought, and *The Exorcist* was damaged in all the 'excellent bits'. What is a kid supposed to do on his last day of the school holidays?

Jordy hated school. Sure, everyone says they hate school yet their schoolbooks were impeccably presented. Jordy started out keen. His book was neatly labelled and covered in adhesive plastic. A week later seemed a year. Leaky pen, cover missing and I LOVE BOBBY written on every page. For that, Jordy broke all of Jenny's Derwent pencils, except the black one. Jordy was sent to the principal and Jenny was sent to a psychiatrist by her parents. It cost Jenny's parents $2400 in fees to realise she needed a new Derwent pencil set. Secretly, Jordy had written ME TOO on every page of his book.

Jordy scraped moss from the dog kennel with a pen knife while Dirk, the dachshund ran around the Hills Hoist eighteen times or until he choked on the leash. Mrs Townsend and Mrs Barnes chatted over the corrugated fence. Jordy listened to them engage in a conversation about 'new ideas'; the magazine, not the enlightenment. They paused as Mr Townsend left, then Mrs Barnes, (or Jude if she'd borrowed a cup of sugar from you) broke the silence like a hatchet through a half inch skull.

"Don't worry pet. Men have killed for less. It's quite common now."

Barbara raised her head in revelation and spoke to Jude, "Oh, Ted and I? It's kind of like the Christmas tree came down years ago."

Jude interjected, "I read about a woman who stabbed her husband to death with a butcher's knife."

Barbara continued, "Sometimes, when I'm really down I just want out. I want to see some of the things I've only read about."

"In court, she was acquitted of murder on the grounds she was suffering from Pre-Menstrual Tension at the time of the incident. So she should." Jude added with a gleeful tone.

"I know it must seem like mid-life crisis . . . " Barbara replied with a heavy sigh.

Jude conceded, "Then there's the woman who knocked off two husbands with arsenic."

"Oh, he's a good man really, is Ted. Never raised a hand to me." Barbara responded quite oblivious to Jude who cut in.

"The third one didn't die, so he became hospitalized. When they found traces of arsenic, it went to court and the media went ape-shit. The husband testified her innocence. What could they do? Good on 'er."

"We used to have some good barneys though, when it all seemed to matter, and now Jordy seems to hate us," continued Barbara while digging her heel into the red mud.

Dirk, the dachshund runs past yelping with his ears pegged together.

"Oh, where did I go wrong?"

Secretly, Jordy had already prepared a list. He pondered this thought as he swung on the Hill's Hoist bemused.

"He'll go to gaol at this rate," Barbara wailed.

"He'll end up queer if he goes to gaol," Jude says with the wave of her bony index finger.

Both Barbara and Jude nervously flicked through their copies of *New Idea.*

I WAS A TEENAGE YUPPIE

"Unashamedly," Jordy declared as he discovered the New Right. He had a 'no fail' 3-point plan to success. It was quite easy really. He would get a paper round, buy out the other paper rounds and finally use his clout to seek a position on the Board of Directors of News Ltd. Coincidently, Rupert Murdoch was reaching for his heart pills at this very moment.

The late school bus was always full. Jordy loved the feeling of rubbing against the other guys buttocks as he boarded and moved to the back. All the straight guys would tighten their muscles. Jordy loved that. He was already daydreaming that he was running a stick along the corrugated iron fence of the housing estate where he lived. He would run so fast that his hand would become numb from the stick. The bus jolted him out of his dream. Above Jordy, who was now seated, stood Bobby. He was the first guy in class to have hairy armpits and wear an earring in his right ear because he 'didn't care'.

Jordy looked out of the window blushing and remained on the bus when it arrived at his school. He didn't get off until four stops after. Sometimes he would have to walk back from the bus depot or wear an extra baggy jumper. It was that awkward age. On his way to school, Jordy stole a copy of *Gentleman Quarterly* and another magazine with friendly men and advertisements for kinky sex. Jordy circled the ones he'd like to try.

At the public school he attended, Yuppie was equated with gay and graduation was getting a Datsun. After a few weeks, Jordy learnt to throw himself down the stairs so as to minimize the bruising. It was literally with pain that Jordy abandoned his quest for Yuppie status, given his socio-economic reality and the fact he owed his father $12.50.

CURIOUSER AND CURIOUSER

Jordy contemplated suicide but decided to masturbate instead. At this point he heard a rustle in the bushes outside his bedroom window. His neighbour, Mr Barnes was dressed in a clown suit wanking furiously. Jordy was disgusted that a pervert could be doing such a disgraceful act at the same time he was, and clown suits were so cliche. Perhaps there were many perverts masturbating at this very moment. Jordy thought about suicide again and then casually let Dirk, the dachshund, out for a night's jaunt. He would inform his father of this very sick act but first he cleared away his porn.

It was quite unusual for the light of the study to be on this late, thought Jordy who unsuccessfully tried to open the door. He peeped through the keyhole. It was even more unusual that Mr Townsend was studying naked while lying down on what appeared to be a beige coloured inflatable raft of some odd configuration. Jordy did not bother to wake his mother, nobody could. It was odd that his walkman batteries had disappeared that night and a humming could be heard from the master bedroom at various intervals.

Meanwhile, Dirk ripped at Mr Barnes' pants savagely. Jordy selected a AC/DC track on a record and adjusted the stereo to FULL as he turned the house lights on. If this woke mother, it would surely wake Mrs Barnes and Mrs Williams and Mr and Mrs Doriello and the MacPhersons and Miss Trewin. Jordy was very surprised that the Wotherspoons had awoken too. We could not be accused of having an anti-climactic night, Jordy ventured in private thoughts. Suburban life can be fun.

WELCOME TO THE AGE OF QUARREL

Next morning, Mrs Barnes returned her *New Idea, Women's Weekly* and *Woman's Day* magazines she'd borrowed, and a copy of *Cleo* without the centrefold while Mr Barnes extended the fence higher in an interesting attempt at guilt reversal. Mrs Townsend mumbled something about a camel with a broken back and Mr Townsend sent Jordy down to hire a video. In his absence, Jordy's parents changed the locks.

Jordy moved into a house with seven others and by the end of the week he'd forgotten his mother's first name. He wanted to taste the other vices of life after he'd broken free from his previous one of corrugated imprisonment. They would still watch the six o'clock news and vote Labor. In the next months, they wouldn't know their own son. They never did. During this time, he cheated death nearly as much as they cheated life. Jordy wanted to live the life of a Kathy Acker novel. Maybe someone will write about me one day, he thought. Looking down at his spoon, he'd forgotten how much stuff he'd jacked up.

THE IDEOLOGICALLY SOUND HOUSEHOLD

When Jordy checked himself out of hospital, he gave a week's notice to his household in St Kilda. While having coffee in the Black Cat Cafe, his attention was drawn to an advertisement for Share Accommodation stuck on the wall. It radiated charm and so did the household, too much in fact. Anne was a single mother with a little boy, not the precocious type. Bill worked for the AIDS Council and his lover, Michael had just received a grant from the Arts Board. Jordy wanted so much to be like them, he'd even say he loved Mary Poppins as a child. He excused himself and went to the bathroom to throw up. His medication was very strong. Attached to the back of the toilet door was a condom vending machine. After the appropriate networking on their part and lies on his part, Jordy found a place to live.

A week later they received this postcard.

There was nothing left for Jordy as he sat in front of the television of his bed-sit. Perhaps he would actually try death but luckily there was a commercial break and a packet of Tim Tams in the fridge. If he couldn't die, he decided he would get fat. His mother would say he looked healthy and the neighbours would say that he'd just been released from Detox. While consuming a biscuit, a man had his head blown off. The children's hour. "What is the world coming to?" his father would say but only after Hawthorn beat Collingwood in the football.

HOMECOMING (HOLD THE STREAMERS)

He was on a train on the Broadmeadows line so Jordy figured he must be returning home. While walking down his street, the scene resembled a patchwork of greens and yellows with a few timid rose bushes every now and then. Headed toward Jordy was a man dressed in leather possibly with an old score to settle. Bad deal? Money owed? Fucked his boyfriend? Jordy's mind drew a blank response. Bobby had filled out as expected and passed his phone number to Jordy eager to catch up on lost time. Jordy bet six to a half-dozen that they would inevitably fuck each other's brains out.

This was it and Jordy had a paragraph to say it in. He arrived speechless. The dog's kennel was on the roof of the house. The fence next door was scattered on four properties. Jordy skidded on a burnt sausage and started to bawl. He bolted inside to see his father cooking two steaks and Mrs Barnes out cold with a bottle of brandy beside her.

"What happened to Dirk?"

"He ran away," replied his father.

"Oh," said Jordy.

"After your mother left."

When Jordy asked about 'Kinko' Barnes as he had become dubbed, his father looked toward the sky. It seemed he'd doused their backyard barbeque with petrol thinking it was cooking oil. A silly error for a Boy Scout leader, one would think. Jordy didn't want to know anything else at this stage. His father overturned the steaks and spoke to Jordy.

"Welcome home, son."

What an ugly word 'Home' when equated with the state of depression of its inhabitants. Jordy thought deeply about the world. His world. Their world. Our world. Friends as urinals, feminists in a fracas and Mankind and His Blueprint Ideology World Tour. Then the earth coughed and the greenies forced us to use scratchy recycled toilet paper. Oh, how he missed those pastel prints.

JOHN LONIE

Contact

'Everyone wanks', says the fresh graffiti on the back of the door. And below, in what looks like the same hand, is a drawing of a huge hand-held ejaculating cock with, by way of a postscript, 'If this is what you like doing to young spunks, try Michael Travers at the Palms Caravan Park.' Graffiti becomes message.

I'm in the bleached and shabby Spanish-Mission style change sheds at one of the unfashionable beaches on the Sunshine Coast, a place which attracts people who can't afford or who disdain the glitter and brashness of the Gold Coast or Noosa. And these door-messages bring me to life, not so much at the thought of the 'young spunk' as at the pleasant knowledge that up here, I am not alone. Not having seen anyone in the past few days other than the odd cute papa walking his children along the surf beach, I muse on the identity of the author or authors.

Then the thought crosses my mind that this Michael Travers could be advertising on his own behalf. If it be him, there are hundreds of candidates, all looking so alike, you'd be hard-pressed to tell one from another. They're as if factory-made and, up here in pre-migrant Oz, come in two basic colours; light blond and dark blond. The only parts of them grown-up are their huge feet and their dicks and they go around in buzzing swarms of sexual tension, ever-ready to pounce on deviant behaviour by any member. Would one of them be so self-possessed and brave as to break ranks? Hardly.

Then there is The Cute Papa. Down the hill from my family's house is a block of fibro flats, each with a verandah. Every day, in the one nearest to us, I've watched the Cute Papa playing with his two baby children, clad only in shorts and with legs and feet of such perfection as to attract a Michelangelo. Does he realize how beautiful he is? His wife does. She gazes at him with adoration through the large open window from the kitchen. I've seen them both walking along the beach. Her eyes hardly ever leave him. Him? Is he the author?

This fantasy becomes very distracting now for whereas before, I've observed the Cute Papa as one looks at a beautiful painting, now I feel the cutting stab of loneliness which, along with desire, I've repressed these past six days. Six days I can manage. On the seventh, there is no rest. This, Paul, I say to myself as warning, brings on the madness. Leave.

Seconds later, I'm in the water, one eye each on two nieces as they splash about in the small but still powerful waves at the edge of the surf while one hand grabs a little nephew who is a stranger to fear. If I wasn't holding on to him, he'd be happily swept away. He's German, this one. Sharks, says the Oz niece to scare her German cousin. *Der Haifisch kommt,* she calls over to Hans, translating the words to her little brother and the threat. But Hans doesn't scare. Where? he asks me, excited by the prospect of a face-to-face meeting. This attracts more of his cousins, four little Australians who, despite the language barrier, have grabbed every chance to terrify their German cousins with tales of sharks, snakes, spiders and crocodiles. Little do they realise this is just grist to the mill for little Hans who relishes the bit in the Grimm tale about Aschenputtl when the step-sisters have to cut off their big toe and heel to fit their feet into the golden slipper.

It's such an irony that up here on holidays, the children are made my reason-of-being. I'm a modern version of the family aunt. Every family has one, says Charlotte Vale in *Now Voyager.* Once a comfort to aged parents, now, in these less charitable days, I fear we're just a plain never-ending unmarried worry to our mothers and fathers. Unlike selfish Mrs Vale, they want to get us off their hands.

It's out of concern for me that my mother has invented this new reason for my existence. To spend time with my nieces and nephews. It's good for me and the children. My siblings and their spouses have taken this up with enthusiasm. It's all bull of course, because, sick of their children, they are now free to sit up on the beach, smoke fags and gossip while I look after their offspring. And that's exactly what they're doing right now, smoking, gossiping and having 'views'. None of my family is short of a 'view'. Except possibly my younger brother who lives in Germany. He lies a little away from the group and behind the camouflage of his sunglasses, eyes off women younger and prettier than his plump and homely Prussian wife Hannelore. They're here to see if Hannelore would like living in Australia. She is underwhelmed at the moment. Everyone goes about barefoot. It's all a bit Third World for Ajax-clean Hannelore from smart Dahlem in Berlin.

You're great with the kids, says my young sister's American husband, who is keen to add to the family brood now the house is built. After a year here, he's become a passionate Australian even if he does get little things wrong now and then. Yesterday in the fruit shop Byron asked for a kilometre instead of a kilogram of mangoes and then fell into sweet confusion when the children all laughed at him. He tries so hard, he who at first hated the heat and wearing no clothes, so there's hope yet for Hannelore.

Then Hannelore says it too — *Du bist doch fantastisch mit den Kindern, Paul.* It's true, I am good with the children. I love them all and, oddly, quite like them all too, even if the two eldest nieces think me entirely wet. Hans, who is Hannelore's four-year-old son, has firmly claimed me. Mother says we're as thick as thieves. How right she is. I enjoy being Uncle/*Onkel.* In reality, I'm one of them, proof of that being that my room is the children's dormitory, except I'm still in it. My father still wants to know where I'm going, who I'm seeing. Mother gives me chocolates like some little reward for being good. Parents never stop being parents but it's easier when the child is childless.

So we play, all of us, a mad bi-lingual mix with me as the Big Kid, a role reinforced by being the translator when grunts, squeals, shoves, fists and laughter fail to bridge the language barrier. It's one up, all up, so by early evening, everyone is so tired, it's almost one in, all in. Each evening, I've been reading the Grimm's Tales, alternately in English and German, but I'm so stuffed sometimes, I forget which until the offended nationality, jealous of its language rights, protests.

It's a moment like this with the children which chips away the last vestiges of my quaint 70's belief that human nature is not fixed at birth.

That night, the children have turned my room into a fort and capture me. My heart's not in it. I am too conscious of my mask. Before, I didn't care. This is part of the reason for holidaying with family. I don't have to negotiate my job, lovers or the city but it's the lovers whose presence I now miss with a sudden ache. Being homosexual has removed me from all that surrounds me up here at my family's holiday house. They all know, of course, but 'it' is never mentioned. Once, I would never have put up with being an 'it', then, in those golden days when I holidayed only with my own tribe and whenever I saw my family, I lectured them on the burning issues of the day. I too had 'views'.

I escape torture and further incarceration by reading yet another Grimm story although, because it's a new one, the old Accord of different languages on alternate nights is deemed over and World Wars One and Two break out again. As in the history books, the Huns bite the dust, although predictably, not without causing horrendous damage, mainly because little Hans has whacked his older Oz cousin Peter on the nose and blood is well and truly spilt. All to no avail. I continue in English as a sop to the wounded Peter. It's the one about the poor fisherman who hauls in a halibut with magic powers. The fisherman's greedy wife forces him to ask the fish for ever more and more until, after he's turned her into the Pope, she asks to become Almighty God himself. The fish turns her back into a harping *hausfrau*, sitting in her pig-pen hovel. Be satisfied with your lot, children, I say as I escape.

My exit from the house is thwarted by my mother telling me to play Scrabble with them. I feel like a walk, I say. Nonsense, she says and sets up a chair. Now play seriously, she admonishes me, because I keep putting out words like 'was' and 'but' and 'and'. There's no point in doing something unless you put your heart and soul into it, she adds. I'm trying, Mother, I reply. God how I'm trying but you keep getting in my way, I add to myself.

Finally, I walk along the beach. It's about 10 o'clock. Out at sea, the lights flash on the shipping buoys and then, around the point, comes a large container ship, all lit up like a passenger liner. The boats come in quite close to the shore as they make their way up and down to the port. At night, you can hear the throb of their engines across the water. I stand and watch it sail by, so near it tantalizes me with thoughts of where it's come from and where after here, it goes. The world, my world.

It's dark tonight. There's no moon but the change sheds are open and lit. I dawdle about by the pool. An old lady swims freestyle so slowly that she must sink but doesn't. She's the only one about. I go into the sheds, heart pounding. It's an age since I've done this and I'm reminded of why I used to do it myself — excitement, pure and simple. A single light bulb shines weakly. No one in the shower room. Further along to the toilets and I can see no-one there and I relax some as expectation and fantasy fade. I push open the door and go inside to review the messages.

The one about Michael Travers is gone. The dick is still there with its 'Everyone wanks' motto. But up the top, maybe in the same hand, is a new message. 'Any sex here over the holidays?' 'Yes', I scrawl under the message, annoyed that I've missed him. Him, I keep thinking of the author as 'him'. I wonder if I might give 'him' a name. But if it is Michael Travers he already has an identity. I'm hoping it's not so I decide to keep thinking about 'him'. The space where the Michael Travers message had been seems terribly blank now. I'm disappointed in a way except it is proof that this door is still in print. I wonder if, thinking he'd been advertising long enough, he removed the message himself. Or what if his father had seen it and rubbed it out and then gone home and rubbed Michael Travers out. Or what . . . I stop this silliness and add to my 'yes' on the wall, 'Tuesday night, after 10.' Then I look at it and think I am headed for purgatory. Fancy me writing messages on toilet walls. It's ludicrous and I laugh. But oh, I am consumed by curiosity and by need of my own kind, even a glance, a smile. Recognition.

Back home, my room is covered with sleeping children and I resent their presence greatly. They smell of children, a mixture of milk and sweat and shit. This is driving me spare. I can't sleep so I read but not very successfully as the night with its heat and humidity calls. Sweaty weather.

Next morning, one up, all up. Aren't you taking the kids down to the beach? my eldest brother asks with an injured tone as I head out the door solo. No, I snap and leave. It's very early and I walk around the headland and along the beach which stretches white and unbroken almost all the way up to Noosa 30 or 40 kilometres away. I haven't been here for years. There used to be an old shipwreck on this beach which in our childhood was still quite substantial. You could climb up the stern quite safely and at low tide, see the rusty propeller sticking out of the sand.

But now, I see it's reduced to some rusted ribbing sticking out of the sand, not, as a fisherman tells me, wholly because of Mother-Sea. Mostly because of souvenir hunters over the past few years. How dare they. We loved that wreck, my cousin and I. We'd sit on the stern and talk till the waves nearly washed us off. And we'd spin marvellous fantasies of what we'd do when we grew up. I look at this wreckage of a wreck and think sourly, bits of my past are sitting in some suburban living room, pathetic relic of a holiday in Queensland. I feel more and more pessimistic about 'people' and in so doing, become more and more my parents' son.

Further along the beach, past where until the 70's, civilisation ended but which now has houses, I walk up into the sand dunes and into the bosky softness of the banksias and casuarinas which, miracle of miracles, still stand guard against the encroachments of the Pacific and the depredations of the greedy. There is one old banksia in particular — I think it is the one — and I sit on its lower trunk. The sun's light dapples the ground and in the familiar mix of the slightly rank smell of the cool sand and the spiciness of the decaying casuarina needles on the ground, I smell memory.

My cousin and I, he nearly 16, a year older than me, would get up at 4.30 in the morning, just before the mid-summer sun peeked over the Pacific horizon. We wore nothing but our Speedos with T-shirts to ward off the morning chill and we carried an air rifle to shoot cane toads because we hated them. They had been responsible for poisoning one of our dogs, so had to be exterminated. But we'd soon get sick of potting these unpottable monsters and go down to the top of the dunes to watch the sun come up. Then Alex would take a small jar of Vaseline from the rifle bag, grease up his erection and fuck me. I remember the delight of the dawn, the sun just warm enough to tingle the skin, the chill of the soft sand under my back, the magpies and currawongs singing and Alex lifting my legs and entering me slowly. He never looked at me. He'd always look ahead, out to the sea. I'd look at him all the time.

The first time, I was amazed. I was lying on the sand looking up at the sky. Without a word, he knelt in front of me, peeled my Speedos from me which exposed my own excitement, lifted my legs and was in. I must have felt very calm and relaxed with him that first time because it didn't hurt — on the contrary. But the second time, it did and it was a little while before it became easy and just like that first time, which dazed me with its intensity. It never worried me that Alex didn't ever look at me. It never crossed my mind that it was odd. He always sensed where I was for we always came together. I recognised him as being in charge and he was.

Afterwards, he'd stay where he was, his eyes closed, his hands holding my feet against his shoulders, me lying before him so light and tranquil that I might have floated away except I was earth bound by his cock inside me. Mostly, we'd start again for that is the age of the permanent erection. Then, down to the water and we'd body-surf together in the waves before running home. By then, everyone would be up and mother would be preparing breakfast. She called us her morning glow-worms because, she said, we glowed after our early morning frolics in the water.

It went on for just over three years, mostly during our holidays, May, August then Christmas, sometimes Easter. I didn't see much of Alex back home because we went to different schools. Alex boarded at Geelong because his parents were diplomats although on his freedom weekends — as he called them — he came to us. Then we'd do it a lot, hidden in the bush down in the Yarra Bend National Park not far from home. Once, in mid-flight, we saw what could have been a tiger snake a few metres away, its head raised slightly, staring at us in shocked amazement like some reptilian schoolmaster. We laughed so much, we both lost our erections. With Alex, I felt fearless.

The beginning of 1969. Alex was just 18 and he was to go back down to Melbourne for his matriculation results. The day he was to leave, we went out before dawn. For over a year now, we'd ignored the cane toads and the air rifle was quietly rusting in a cupboard. We walked along the beach and back, hardly a word between us. We went to our spot and he fucked me twice. After the second time, I remember looking up at him and glorying in how handsome he was, such long dark eye-lashes, dark hair and olive skin — my brothers and sister and I were all fair and looked just like every other teenager in our narrow world. But Alex didn't. I realised just how much I worshipped him. And then he so surprised me by saying something. I must have looked puzzled because he looked down at me and smiled. He'd said my name and he said it again as he nuzzled his face against my feet which were resting on his shoulders. Then he kissed my left foot before gently letting my legs down and helping me up. He gazed at me, lifting his hand to stroke my cheek. At that moment, he looked right into me, and had he said, run away with me to sea or fly with me to the moon, death alone would have stopped me. Then, he sighed and something changed in his eyes, I can't remember exactly except that the intense contact was gone. Suddenly he tweaked my nose and raced off to the water, calling on me to follow. I remember I had an almost uncontrollable urge to burst into tears for I must have sensed what had happened.

Married with a young family, at the Victorian Bar, a successful barrister, I've hardly seen him since. And now, as I savour the memory, I don't want to move. I close my eyes and there's an unspoken wish to return to childhood, my childhood, to this spot 20 years back, for while I couldn't have realised it at the time, in those few years, I was content as I've never been since.

You are very distant? says Hannelore as she irons the bedsheets. She's the only one who notices I'm not my sunny self. No, I reply, just a bit flat. Ach, she says sagely in German, here with your family and you are lonely. She's quite right and I recoil at the touch of her words. The only thing keeping me from hopping on the sparkling new ICE-Train down to Brisbane and a plane south is curiosity about tonight's rendezvous at 10pm.

I wonder what brings me here, what on earth joins me to my mother and father. Parents and children are only accidentally related, says hunchbacked Rhoda to her accidental brother Hurtle in *The Vivisector*. If we are all reincarnated, then my parents as well as being the genetic means for this incarnation, are also possibly my trial and I am theirs. If so, I'm doing much better than they are.

Such a long face, my mother says to me. Help me wipe up. So I do. She talks about a poorly lemon-scented gum in her garden. Mother's trees. We have a lot of land here and over the years Mother has planted trees from all over tropical Australia. From using them as childhood playthings to student cynicism about her motive for planting them — merely to improve the worth of the property — Mother's trees are now genuinely absorbing for me. They are one thing we actually can share. I say I'll help her lop some of the diseased branches.

Hans is at me to go to the rock pools to watch the crabs scuttle away as he stomps Germanically into their homes. Hans can only be a little poofter-basher in training and if I were truly mindful of my tribe's well-being, I should let him fall in and drown. But he fascinates me more than any of the others for the very reason we are attracted by the archetypal Young Australian Male which even though he's German and four, little Hans, in behaviour, resembles alarmingly. A friend of mine refers to them derisively as Yams.

They are good-looking of course with the beauty of youth but it is their energetic maleness which is fascinating, although for us, that is a bit like the lethal fascination the snake has for the hapless frog. Social class is at work too and even if I do scoff at the English Grands like those characters of E M Forster's fantasies, aristos who can find fulfilment only with the under-gamekeeper, I too have fantasised about being scooped up by some smudgy mechanic and loved senseless. The Cute Papa will do very nicely. But there's not the remotest chance I would allow it. It's sad, I think sometimes, that with growing older, one becomes wise to the idiocy of falling for the sort of beauty which, you find out all too quickly, does indeed have the intelligence of a yam. So, I mightn't be the snake but I certainly am no frog. I observe Hans and his ilk for the most part, quite dispassionately.

Off we go, the girls their own gaggle and me with the boys. The rocks are slippery. This deters the girls who collect shells on the sand. The older boys climb the cliff-face. I have Hans who is not deterred by slippery rocks although he does show unusual wisdom in holding firmly onto my hand. We could both go, I think.

Hans is thoroughly absorbed by the tiny fish and the crabs until, suddenly, let's kill them, he shouts, with Teutonic relish. This after I've been telling him about the wonders of life, of conservation, of loving all creatures. But all that's as water off a duck's back to this little von Moltke. What counts is I'm bigger than he is and I say I'll give him a clout on the ear if he so much as raises his little finger against a sandfly. Good old violence. Oddly, a whack on the ear doesn't sound at all impressive in German but it works all the same.

A gangly teenager, 15 or 16, lolls about in the large rock pool. He's all arms and legs. I notice him because he is by himself. That is rare up here. You belong to a swarm or you're dead. It was like that when I was his age except we were self-contained, my brothers and cousins and our house was away from the town. We were called then 'the Victorians' by the locals because in those days, we were the only ones.

The gangly boy gets out of the rock pool and sits on the sand nearby where his towel and belongings are. He lights a cigarette which he smokes self-consciously and then I notice he's holding the silly thing between his middle and third fingers. He sees me looking at him and he grins and I say g'day. He nods his head, still grinning and says hallo — not the ubiquitous 'hi' but 'hallo'. If he were a member of a swarm, he'd scowl in self-defence and start chewing his finger-nails. I'm very tempted to say, are you Michael Travers? Then Hans falls into the rock pool and yells blue murder that he's all wet. The little bugger is only attention-getting but, *in loco parentis,* I scoop him out and take him home to change. Why Hannelore didn't put his swimmers on, I don't know. The gangly teenager watches me as I go. See ya, he says and coolly draws on his fag, as if he were in a 30's film doing cigarette-acting.

Who's that? Hans demands. Who? I ask. Him, he says unexpectedly in English, pointing at the gangly teener. One of the boys who went away with the Pied Piper from Hamelin, I spin and go on to tell him the horrors they went through before they came to Australia where they're now living happily ever after. Hans is utterly absorbed by my explanation and forgets to whinge that he's wet. He repeats the bare bones to Hannelore when we get home, the really horrible bits of course, and she casts a baleful look in my direction.

I sit on the balcony. I'm convinced now that Him has to

be that lad and that he probably is Michael Travers. Just my luck and if he's there tonight, what on earth am I going to do? I won't go, I say to myself, quite certain of course that nothing on Earth will keep me away from satisfying, at least my curiosity. But what will I do? Knock him off? Give him a good time? Something to remember and look for again? A role model? Didn't I, doesn't every gay boy, dream of being found by an attractive man and taken off to paradise?

Yet I'm no missionary. Slaking his desire, I may feed his soul. But what about me? I feel at the moment only the sort of desire that makes one quite undiscriminating. More madness. Maybe I'll get my brother to drive me over to Nambour to the ICE-Train and I can be back home by tonight.

Night. Story time is over quickly because if it isn't, I'll bloody smother you — in English and German. At 9.45 I go for a walk. In the distance along the beach, I see figures at the pool and my heart tightens as I think, ah, right, it's all a poofter-bashers' ploy and I'm about to walk right into their trap. The snake has me in its grip however and I trot along the beach, pretending to be a late-night jogger.

The figures around the pool are the old lady from before and an even older-looking gentleman, both so wizened, they look just like frill-necked lizards. They're leaving as I come up to the pool. Nice evening, I say in shaky voice. Yairs, they both say as they toddle away. Very nice. 9.58 and I'll explode. No one about so I quickly go in through the portals and into the mens' change rooms, heart almost stopping. It's exciting and I'm loving every second of the anticipation.

No one. Empty. Nothing. I push open the door. 'Please, can only do daytime', says the message under my 'meet you at ten'. God save me. It is that wretched teenager. Any wimp can sneak out at night. What's wrong with him! So could the Cute Papa. I'm furious. The only way to calm down is to take off all my clothes and swim back and forth in the pool. I do at least a kilometre.

It's always like this, I grumble. If it were my friend and ex, Wolfgang, the place would be awash with men. No matter where we went, some chap would pop out of the woodwork. Of all the unlikely places, Leningrad once, a soldier in the Red Army, though not, it has to be said, in uniform which disappointed Wolf greatly. Words failed me at the time as they did when, after I'd left Germany for home and he'd followed me out here, we were on our way to Adelaide in the car and pulled into a motel in the middle of a desert and sure enough, as soon as Wolf got out of the car, out popped an attractively moustached face. But now he has the bug and I am grateful each day the bug doesn't have him because I love him. He's away in the snow in Enzed with his boyfriend, pretending he's 20 and back in Kitz-buehel.

My single bed surrounded by a sea of sleeping children, I sleep on the unfairness of life soothed only by the scent from mother's eucalypts which the night breeze wafts in through the open window.

'Please, can only do daytime.' It's not just a message for a possible rendezvous, it's the tribal calling card, and even if our affections in lonely places like this are mediated by cock — and what's wrong with that — we have the affection of one of our own, however fleeting. And if you are 16 or 66, it will please you and make you feel less alone. Am I indeed to be a missionary or is it social worker? Whoever Him is, there's Life out there and I am its representative here and now. Grab a sample. Oh loneliness, we know all about loneliness, about sitting with your family and not being able to tell the truth.

The sun is hardly up. '2 pm today', I write on the door and leave. Children, parents, brothers and sisters and the whole caboodle snooze then. So does the whole town for at long last, Whitey accepts he lives in the tropics and not in Europe.

After breakfast, having decided the *eucalyptus citriadora* is not long for the world, Mother asks me to help her plant another, which we do. Nothing is said as we dig the hole, prepare it and put the sapling in. I enjoy the ritual and so does she. There, isn't that nice, she says happily and I realize it is not just the tree-planting she means. It's also my being there in both spirit as well as body. It's simple really. I give her happi-ness and pleasure by helping her plant the tree, simply by being there. I realize she knows when I am not there and it must trouble her because her concern is for me to be happy. You'll be terribly lonely, she said to me years ago when I told her. We walk among her trees and she says, the trees keep me company, you know.

It's two o'clock in the change room and I change into my swimmers. The gangly lad from the rock pool, bold as brass, strides in. He grins. I laugh. Not here, he says and beckons me to follow. Madness. I follow.

Over the hill and into the bush until he stops in a quiet secluded spot. How old are you? I ask. Nineteen, he says. Bull, I say. Seventeen, he corrects and I still think he's lying. He drops his shorts and steps out of them, his erection springing up and flapping against his tummy. Fool, I say to myself. I've built up to this rendezvous, I've walked all this way with him, what else is he going to expect. The madness has brought you to this idiocy. Hang on honey, I say and put a paternal hand to his face. I am about to say you're too young for me and I'm too old for you when I feel him trembling under my touch and he puts his hand up to my hand and presses it against his cheek. My heart melts. He's scared, so scared he's shaking, and I realize that it is he who's taken the huge risk, not me. I fold him in to me and hold him and he hangs on tightly, so tightly.

His erection hasn't gone away and then he shudders and grabs me hard as I feel him come against my thigh. I hold him tight and press my face to his, stroking the back of his neck and head. Then I feel dampness on my cheek and he's crying softly. It's okay, I say quietly, hoping he feels safe with me, cry all you want. And he does.

For ages, we stand there, him hanging on tight. I can hear his heart beat and the sound of the blood coursing through his veins, this stranger. I should be looking after him, not that little thug Hans or any of my nieces and nephews. They've got their parents. This one, he's my tribe, that's for sure. Who looks after him? Who looks after any of us at that time?

I use my handkerchief and dry his eyes which are bloodshot. I kiss him on the cheek and motion to him to sit down. I cover his nakedness with my towel. He takes out his cigarettes and offers me one and I accept, even though I don't smoke. He lights us up and I have him lean against me as I lean against the soft trunk of a large paperbark. I can smell the pungent sweetness of its flowers.

Here on holidays, he lives in an inland coal town, up north on the Tropic of Capricorn. He's doing matric, is nearly 18 and now I believe him. To me, anyone under 25 looks 16. He hopes to go to university in Brisbane next year. I tell him how brave he is, taking such a chance. So are you, he says, we're illegal up here, you know. Not 'it's' illegal but 'we're' illegal. He is so lonely, so very lonely, you can taste the need on his skin.

Multiply him by thousands and what other way is there than the change rooms or a public toilet whose doors become a *samizdat?* And when as strangers we collide in that fleeting moment, the immensity of feeling between us creates such a closeness that we go on searching for it, desperate just once more to taste the sweetness it brings. It surely is the kindness of strangers.

I tell him my name. What's yours? I ask, knowing the answer full well. But so much for that because, David, he replies, David Franken.

gangsters by day, girls by night

Tina had been in and out of prisons since she was fifteen. Her first escape was so daring that the media had built her into a giant in the wake of the manhunt which had led to her recapture.

Actually she was barely over five foot tall, petite, waiting for release so that she could have an operation to become a woman and marry her boyfriend, also a prisoner. The first guy that tried to rape her in prison bashed her so badly in the attempt that sex was impossible. When he went to sleep, she took to him with a wooden stool. He was hospitalised and after that her reputation as a 'maddy' made her safe.

When she was out she wore Barbara Streisand drag to the best hotels and restaurants for dinners on the proceeds of her many armed robberies.

She had plenty of sex in jail and usually she was the active partner. As we walked around the exercise yard together she pointed out one guy after another and finally to the biggest guy who was working out with weights.

"Him?" I asked incredulously.

"Him," she shrieked.

But he's such a stud, I thought to myself.

She was reading my mind.

"Around here darling," she giggled, "they're all gangsters by day and girls by night."

Contributor Notes

Tony Ayres is a freelance screenwriter/director. Most recently he has directed a short documentary for the UK Channel 4 series *Out on Tuesday*, about gay and lesbian Aborigines. His television play, *Loveless*, about fathers, sons and sex, is in production for the SBS drama series *Six Pack*. Tony was born in Macau, but has been in Australia since he can remember.

Kerry Bashford is an editor of *Pink Ink: a lesbian and gay anthology* and *hell bent* magazine. He's supposed to be writing a novel that he intends passing off as a thesis. He doesn't know which it will be or what it's about but he'll keep on writing until he comes up with thirty thousand fabulous words.

Benedict Ciantar is 26 and currently holidaying in the Northern Hemisphere but plans to be back later this year, in time for the launching of his first novel *Distractions*.

Kosta Matsoukas is Greek by birth, nomad by temperament, academic philospher by training, cultural activist given half a chance, a gay father, unmarried on principle, compulsively individualist, prefers the ocean to the mountains; not a humble man.

A television baby from Cronulla, **Tim Herbert** has been a bank clerk, book seller, tutor, cleaner and editor. His stories have been published in several gay publications and the now remaindered *Fictions 88*. At present he is co-editing a new anthology of S & M fiction entitled *Love Cries*.

Sasha Soldatow currently resides in Moscow.

Mark Try is a Sydney writer whose stories have appeared in a number of magazines and the anthology *Ink — The Follow Me Collection*. He is an ex-editor of both *Campaign* and *Hermes* and currently lives in London.

Ian MacNeill has written, from a gay perspective, articles and essays, fiction, poetry and drama. *TV Tricks*, a collection of his poetry, was published by *BlackWattle Press* in 1989. *Libbing*, a collection of articles was published by *Mieli Press* in 1990.

Gary Dunne's short stories, reviews and articles have been appearing in magazines and anthologies since the late seventies. He was one of the editors of the gay and lesbian anthology *Edge City on Two Different Plans* in 1983 and has published two collections of fiction, *If Blood Should Stain the Lino* (1983) and *As If Overnight* (1990). He lives in Sydney's inner west with a lesbian porn writer and her geriatric dog.

Denis Gallagher was born in Sydney in 1948. He is the author of four books of poetry; *International Stardom* (1977), *Country, Country* (1979), *Making Do* (1982), and *These Tattoos* (1990), as well as a book of short stories, *Two Stories* (1982). In 1987 he compiled, edited and published the anthology, *Love and Death*.

Giles Hugo was born in South Africa but settled in Tasmania five years ago. His stories have appeared in several magazines including *Australian Short Stories* and *Cargo*. He is currently preparing his novel *Leper's Kiss* for publication.

Edward McCann dislikes the appellation 'Gay writer'. Also Heterosexual, Bisexual, Monosexual, Homosexual or Asexual. He believes acceptance of these designations puts a person into a box — thus inhibiting exploration of the rich, and varied tapestry of one's sexuality. This makes him a very difficult person to live with.

Graeme Aitken writes a regular literary column for the *Sydney Star Observer*, and has had several stories published in Sydney based magazines. He is 27 and originally from NZ.

Mikey Haliday was born in 1966, Adelaide. He has completed a BA (Communications) at the University of Technology, Sydney. His first story, *Kina Gods* won the youth award in the 1990 *OutRage* Short Story Competition. As well as writing for gay publications, Mikey is also an editor of *Pink Ink* and appears as Boy Sprout in a comic strip in the magazine *hell bent*. He is writing his first novel.

John Lonie is a script-writer who lives in Sydney and whose most recent major work was the 1990 mini-series *The Paper Man* for ABC television. He currently story-lines and edits for *A Country Practice* and has a new mini-series *Frankie's House* due to start filming in late 1991.

Michael White's book of short stories *gangsters by day, girls by night*, was published in 1990, a few weeks before his death from an AIDS related illness.

BlackWattle Press Books

Available from good bookstores, or
direct from BWP (Australian postage paid)

GARY DUNNE — As If Overnight
'Until last year, we were like Peter Pan and the Lost Boys. Now
we are blatantly mortal. It's as if we've changed overnight
and we will never be young again.'
From the author of *If Blood Should Stain the Lino*
Novella, 32 pages, Sept 1990, ISBN 1.875243.01.1, RRP $7.00

DENIS GALLAGHER — These Tattoos
Denis is already the author of several books of poetry. *These
Tattoos* is a selection of his writing from 1975 to 1990.
From the Author of *Making Do*
Poetry, 44 pages, Sept 1990, ISBN 1.875243.02.X, RRP $7.00

IAN MACNEILL — TV Tricks and other poems
For more than a decade Ian's poetry and short stories have
been published by Australian magazines much to the
enjoyment of his readers. This, his first book, presents all
new work over a variety of themes.
From the author of *Libbing*
Poetry, 48 pages, June 1989, ISBN 1.875243.00.3, RRP $7.00

SASHA SOLDATOW — The Adventures of Rock'n'roll Sally
A chronicle of life in the seventies and all that was. Sally's
career is portrayed vividly through life and love.
'It's raunchy, vicious, funny and camp' Robert Dessaix
From the author of *Private - do not open*
Performance, 32 pages, Sept 1990, ISBN 1.875243.04.6, RRP $7.00

MICHAEL WHITE — Gangsters by Day, Girls by Night
'Michael White's first book is full of stories and observations of
inner city life and personal experiences . . . his work will
thrill with his swift flow of words and sense of humour . . .
the stories read like dinner party pieces, polished to
perfection, delivered by an accomplished raconteur.'
Sydney Star Observer. A best seller.
Short Stories, 64 pages, Dec 1990, ISBN 1.875243.05.4, RRP $9.50

BlackWattle Press

PO Box 4, Leichhardt NSW 2040